S0-BQH-630

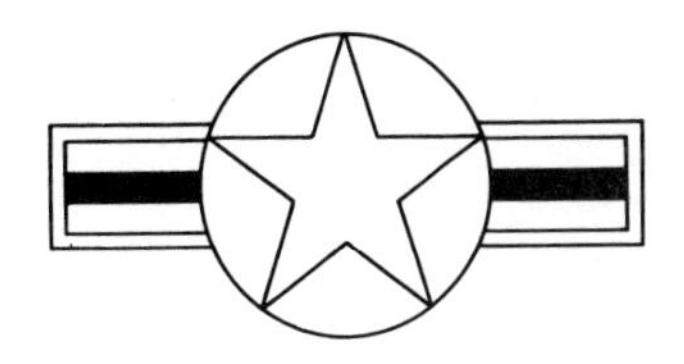

The
United States
in
World War II

THE UNITED STATES IN WORLD WAR II

Illustrated
with
photographs,
and maps
by
Robert Standley

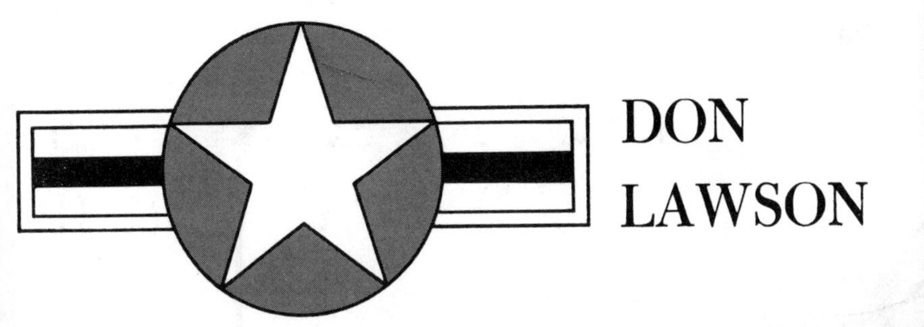

DON LAWSON

Crusade for World Freedom

Abelard - Schuman
London
New York
Toronto

Library of Congress Catalogue Card Number: 63-16225

LONDON	NEW YORK	TORONTO
Abelard-Schuman Limited	Abelard-Schuman Limited	Abelard-Schuman Canada Limited
8 King St. WC2	6 West 57th St.	896 Queen St. W.

Printed in the United States of America
Designed by The Etheredges

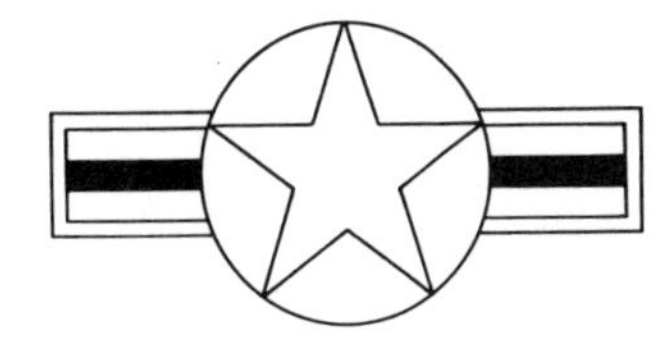

To
Sergeant
George Borger,
Sergeant
R. W. Cannon,
and
to the memory of
our great
good friend,
Sergeant
Kenneth Brown

Acknowledgments

The author is greatly indebted to several persons for their assistance in the preparation of this book. Harold Kolom was most cooperative in giving me an eyewitness account of the Japanese attack on Bellows Field, Hawaii. I wish to thank him also for letting me reproduce his historic letter written on Sunday morning, December 7, 1941.

Wayne Hartwell, Editorial Librarian, *Compton's Pictured Encyclopedia*, was once again a great aid in research and in preparing the bibliography. I also wish to thank Verne Pore for preparing the index, and Eleanor Brooks for typing the final manuscript.

The Army, Navy, Air Force, and National Archives were most generous in supplying photographs. Major Gene Gurney and Alice Martin of the United States Air Force Book Program were especially helpful in this regard.

Grateful acknowledgment is made to the following publishers for permission to use excerpts from books on their lists:

A History of the United States Air Force, copyright 1957 Air Force Association, courtesy of D. Van Nostrand Company, Inc.

Black Thursday by Martin Caidin, E. P. Dutton & Co., Inc.

Five Down and Glory by Gene Gurney, G. P. Putnam's Sons, copyright 1958 by Gene Gurney and Mark P. Friedlander, Jr.

The Marauders by Charlton Ogburn, Jr., Harper and Row.

THE WAR A Concise History 1939-45 by Louis L. Snyder, copyright 1960 by Louis L. Snyder, permission granted by Julian Messner, Inc.

Wake Island Command by W. Scott Cunningham, Little, Brown and Company.

The story about the Corregidor flag is adapted from *The Compact History of the U.S. Army* by Col. R. Ernest Dupuy, USA (Ret.) copyright 1956, 1961 by Hawthorn Books, Inc. The Sultan of Morocco's quotation about General Patton is reprinted from this same source.

The story about Sergeant McKeogh and other direct quotations about General Dwight D. Eisenhower are from *Crusade in Europe* by Dwight D. Eisenhower, copyright 1948 by Doubleday and Company, Inc., reprinted by permission of the publisher.

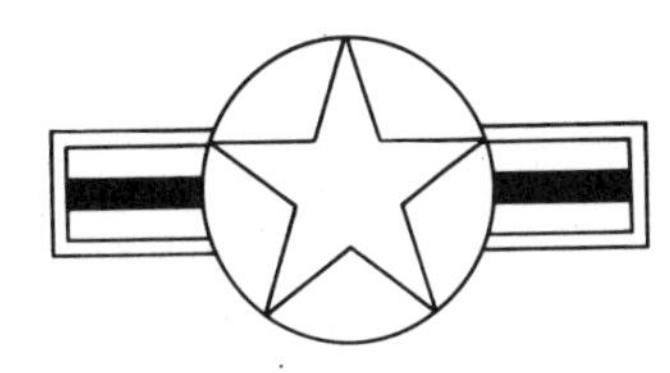

Contents

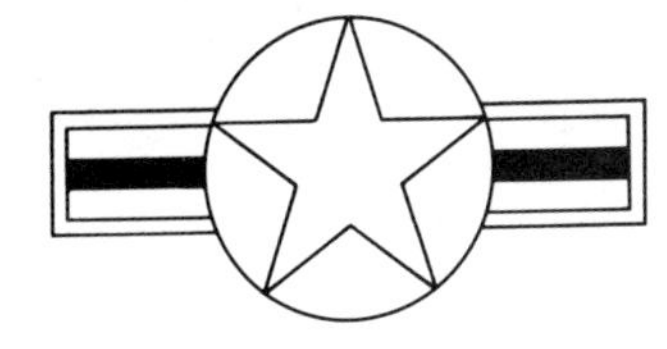

Illustrations

MAPS

PHOTOGRAPHS

World War II
Table
of Events

1939

September	*1*	Germany invades Poland.
September	*3*	Britain and France declare war on Germany.
September	*27*	Warsaw falls to Germans.
October	*14*	British battleship *Royal Oak* sunk at Scapa Flow.
November	*30*	Russia invades Finland.
December	*17*	Captain Langsdorff scuttles *Graf Spee* at Montevideo, Uruguay.

1940

March	*12*	Finland and Russia sign peace treaty.
April	*9*	Germany occupies Denmark and Norway.
May	*10*	Churchill becomes British prime minister. Germany invades Belgium, Luxemburg, and the Netherlands.
May	*14*	Surrender of the Netherlands.
May	*28*	Belgium surrenders.
June	*4*	"Miracle of Dunkirk" completed.
June	*10*	Italy declares war on Britain and France.
June	*22*	France surrenders to Germany.
June	*24*	France surrenders to Italy.
August	*12*	Battle of Britain begins.
September	*3*	Fifty destroyers traded by U.S. to Britain for naval and air bases.

October	*31*	Battle of Britain ends in RAF victory. Night "blitz" of London and other British cities continues.

1941

March	*11*	Lend-Lease Act signed by Roosevelt.
May	*24*	British ship, *Hood,* sunk by German ship, *Bismarck.*
May	*27*	*Bismarck* sunk by British.
June	*22*	Germany invades Russia.
December	*7*	Japanese attack Pearl Harbor.
December	*8*	United States and Britain declare war on Japan.
December	*11*	Germany and Italy declare war on the United States, and the United States in turn declares war.
December	*23*	Wake Island falls to Japanese.

1942

February	*15*	Singapore falls to Japanese.
March	*13-17*	MacArthur escapes to Australia from Philippines.
April	*9*	Bataan falls to Japanese.
April	*18*	Doolittle flyers raid Tokyo.
May	*6*	Corregidor surrenders.
May	*4-8*	Battle of the Coral Sea stops Japanese southeastward conquest.
June	*3-6*	Battle of Midway: turning point of the war in the Pacific.
June	*25*	Eisenhower and staff arrive in England.
July	*1*	Germans stopped by British at El Alamein: turning point in the war for Britain.
July	*4*	First U.S. Eighth Air Force flyers bomb Europe.
August	*7*	Battle of Guadalcanal begins.
August	*19*	Dieppe raided by Commandos and Rangers.

August	*24*	Siege of Stalingrad begins.
November	*8*	U.S. forces invade North Africa.
November	*13-15*	Japanese naval forces defeated by U.S. Navy off Guadalcanal.

1943

January	*14-24*	Casablanca conference; "unconditional surrender" terms announced.
February	*2*	Russians lift German siege of Stalingrad: turning point of war on the Eastern front.
February	*8*	Guadalcanal campaign ends in complete U.S. victory.
February	*21*	U.S. soldiers defeated at Kasserine Pass.
May	*12*	Last of Germans driven out of Africa.
June	*4*	American forces begin year-long advance along northern shores of New Guinea.
July	*10*	Allies invade Sicily.
July	*25*	Mussolini forced to resign.
September	*3*	Allies invade Italy.
September	*9*	U.S. forces hit the beach at Salerno.
September	*16*	U.S. and British forces link up at Salerno.
October	*1*	Naples falls to Allies.
October	*13*	Italy declares war on Germany.
October	*14*	Most savage air battle in history fought by U.S. Eighth Air Force attacking Schweinfurt.
November	*1*	U.S. forces invade Bougainville.
November	*21*	U.S. forces invade Tarawa and Makin islands.

1944

January	*22*	U.S. forces hit the beach at Anzio.
February	*1-5*	U.S. forces capture Kwajalein.

March	*7*	Merrill's Marauders invade Burma.
May	*17*	Marauders capture Myitkyina airfield.
June	*4*	U.S. troops enter Rome: first Axis capital to fall.
June	*6*	D-Day landings in Normandy.
June	*12*	Germans launch buzz bombs against England.
June	*15*	U.S. forces invade Saipan.
August	*1*	Patton's Third Army exploits breakout from Normandy beachhead.
August	*15*	Invasion of Southern France.
August	*17-20*	Battle of the Falaise Gap.
August	*25*	Paris liberated.
October	*20*	U.S. forces invade Leyte.
December	*16-27*	Battle of the Bulge.

1945

January	*9*	MacArthur returns to Philippines as Americans invade Luzon.
February	*19*	U.S. forces invade Iwo Jima.
March	*7*	U.S. forces seize Remagen bridge across Rhine River.
April	*1*	U.S. forces invade Okinawa.
April	*12*	President Roosevelt dies.
April	*28*	Mussolini executed by Italian partisans.
April	*30*	Hitler commits suicide.
May	*1*	German troops surrender in Italy.
May	*7*	Germany surrenders to Allies at Reims.
July	*5*	Philippines liberated.
August	*6*	B-29 Enola Gay drops atomic bomb on Hiroshima.
August	*8*	Russia declares war on Japan.
August	*9*	B-29 Bock's Car drops atomic bomb on Nagasaki.
August	*10*	Japan asks for peace terms.
September	*2*	Japan signs surrender terms.

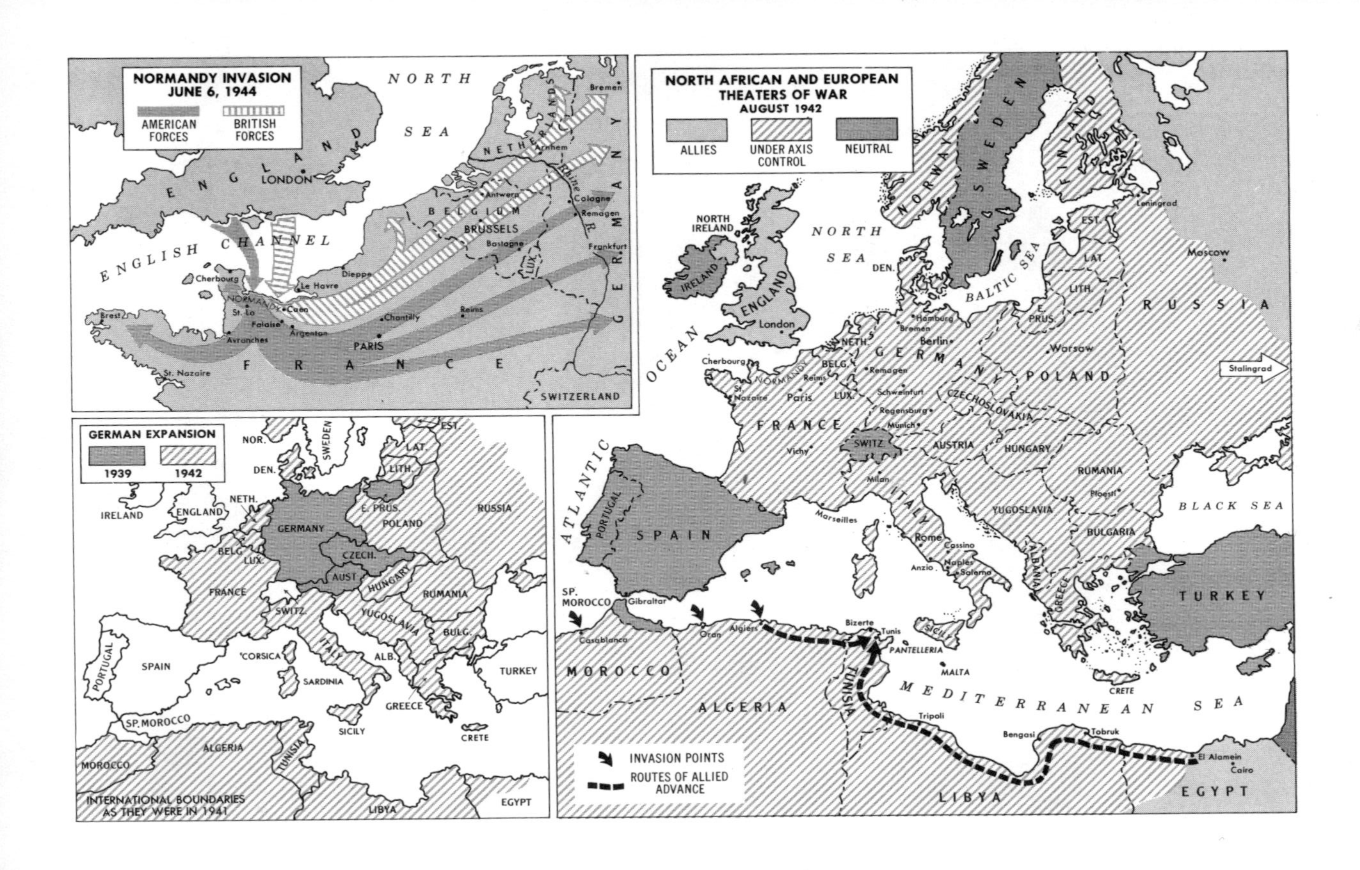
NORMANDY INVASION
JUNE 6, 1944
AMERICAN FORCES
BRITISH FORCES
ENGLAND
LONDON
NORTH SEA
ENGLISH CHANNEL
NETHERLANDS
BELGIUM
BRUSSELS
GERMANY
FRANCE
PARIS
SWITZERLAND
LUX.
Bremen
Arnhem
Rhine R.
Antwerp
Cologne
Remagen
Bastogne
Frankfurt
Dieppe
Le Havre
Cherbourg
NORMANDY
Caen
St. Lo
Falaise
Argentan
Chantilly
Reims
Brest
Avranches
St. Nazaire
GERMAN EXPANSION
1939
1942
NOR.
SWEDEN
EST.
LAT.
LITH.
DEN.
E. PRUS.
POLAND
RUSSIA
IRELAND
ENGLAND
NETH.
GERMANY
BELG.
LUX.
CZECH.
AUST
HUNGARY
RUMANIA
FRANCE
SWITZ.
YUGOSLAVIA
BULG.
PORTUGAL
SPAIN
CORSICA
ITALY
ALB.
TURKEY
SARDINIA
GREECE
SP. MOROCCO
SICILY
CRETE
ALGERIA
MOROCCO
TUNISIA
LIBYA
EGYPT
INTERNATIONAL BOUNDARIES AS THEY WERE IN 1941
NORTH AFRICAN AND EUROPEAN THEATERS OF WAR
AUGUST 1942
ALLIES
UNDER AXIS CONTROL
NEUTRAL
NORWAY
SWEDEN
FINLAND
Leningrad
NORTH IRELAND
IRELAND
ENGLAND
London
NORTH SEA
DEN.
BALTIC SEA
EST.
LAT.
LITH.
Moscow
RUSSIA
E. PRUS.
Hamburg
Bremen
Berlin
OCEAN
NETH.
GERMANY
Warsaw
POLAND
Stalingrad
Cherbourg
NORMANDY
BELG.
Remagen
Reims
Schweinfurt
St. Nazaire
Paris
LUX.
CZECHOSLOVAKIA
Regensburg
Munich
FRANCE
AUSTRIA
HUNGARY
SWITZ.
Vichy
ATLANTIC
RUMANIA
Milan
Ploesti
PORTUGAL
YUGOSLAVIA
BLACK SEA
Marseilles
ITALY
SPAIN
Rome
BULGARIA
Cassino
ALBANIA
Anzio
Naples
Salerno
GREECE
TURKEY
SP. MOROCCO
Gibraltar
Bizerte
Tunis
Casablanca
Oran
Algiers
SICILY
PANTELLERIA
MOROCCO
MALTA
TUNISIA
CRETE
MEDITERRANEAN SEA
ALGERIA
Tripoli
Bengasi
Tobruk
El Alamein
Cairo
INVASION POINTS
ROUTES OF ALLIED ADVANCE
LIBYA
EGYPT

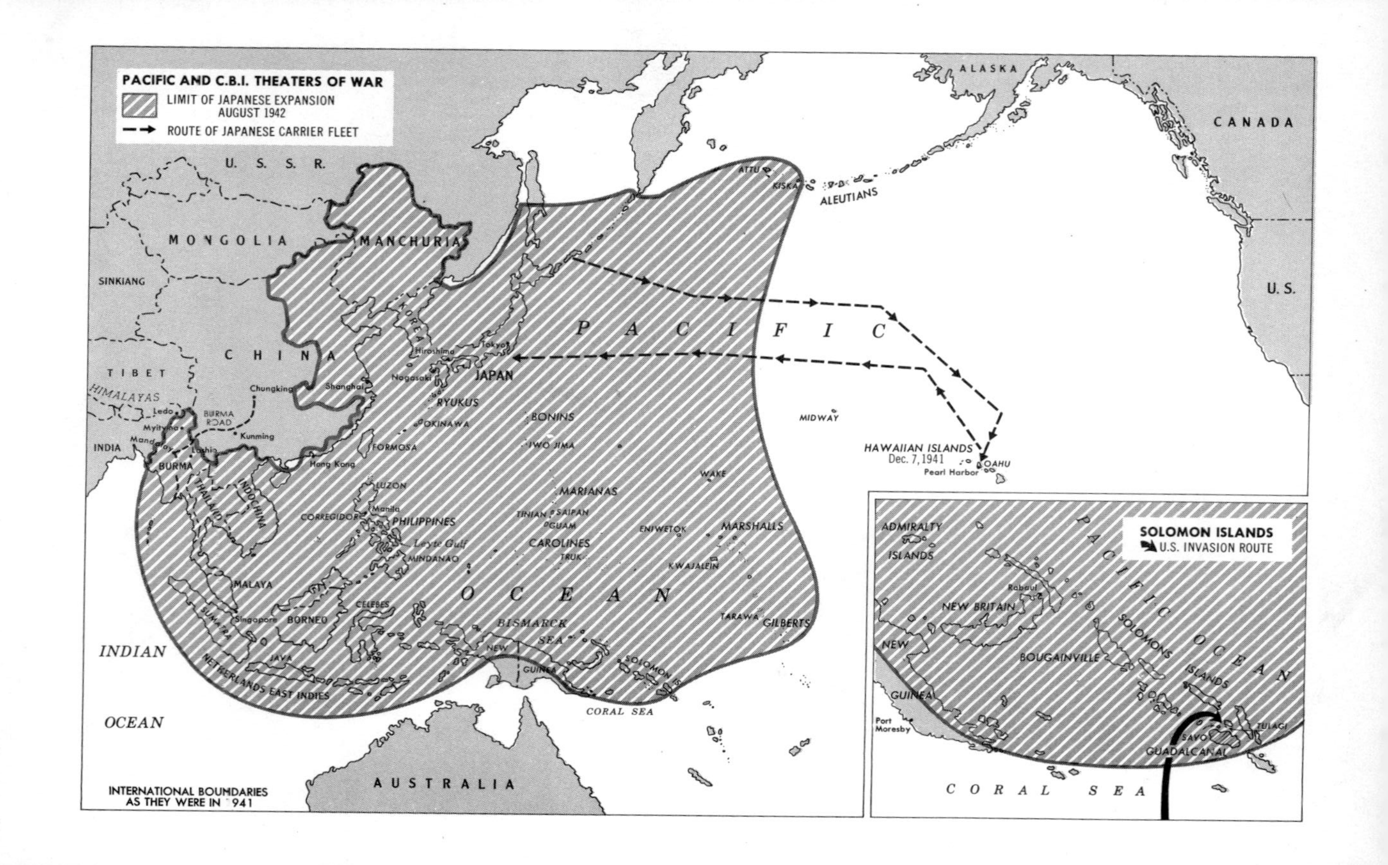
PACIFIC AND C.B.I. THEATERS OF WAR
LIMIT OF JAPANESE EXPANSION AUGUST 1942
ROUTE OF JAPANESE CARRIER FLEET
U. S. S. R.
MONGOLIA
MANCHURIA
SINKIANG
KOREA
CHINA
TIBET
HIMALAYAS
Chungking
Shanghai
Hiroshima
Tokyo
Nagasaki
JAPAN
RYUKUS
OKINAWA
BONINS
IWO JIMA
Ledo
BURMA ROAD
Kunming
INDIA
BURMA
Hong Kong
FORMOSA
THAILAND
INDOCHINA
LUZON
Manila
CORREGIDOR
PHILIPPINES
Leyte Gulf
MINDANAO
MARIANAS
TINIAN
SAIPAN
GUAM
CAROLINES
TRUK
ENIWETOK
MARSHALLS
KWAJALEIN
WAKE
MALAYA
Singapore
SUMATRA
BORNEO
CELEBES
JAVA
NETHERLANDS EAST INDIES
BISMARCK SEA
NEW GUINEA
SOLOMON IS.
CORAL SEA
TARAWA
GILBERTS
P A C I F I C
O C E A N
INDIAN
OCEAN
AUSTRALIA
ATTU
KISKA
ALEUTIANS
ALASKA
CANADA
U.S.
MIDWAY
HAWAIIAN ISLANDS
Dec. 7, 1941
Pearl Harbor
OAHU
INTERNATIONAL BOUNDARIES AS THEY WERE IN 1941
SOLOMON ISLANDS
U.S. INVASION ROUTE
ADMIRALTY ISLANDS
Rabaul
NEW BRITAIN
NEW GUINEA
Port Moresby
BOUGAINVILLE
SOLOMONS
ISLANDS
PACIFIC OCEAN
TULAGI
SAVO
GUADALCANAL
CORAL SEA

One

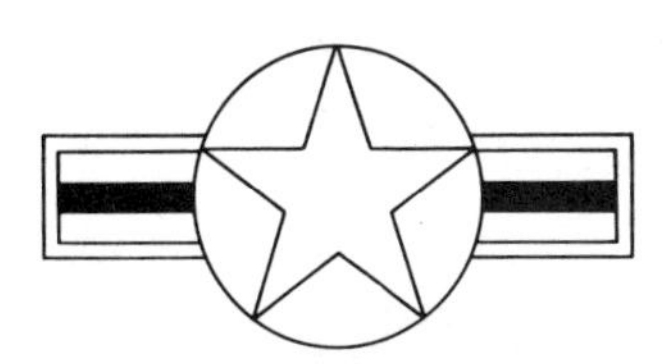

"Remember Pearl Harbor!"

In the dark and lonely predawn hours of Sunday morning, December 7, 1941, two sleepy-eyed United States Army privates sat watching the screen of a radarscope on the island of Oahu, Hawaii. The mobile radar set was stationed high on a wooded mountain slope some twenty-five or thirty miles from Fort Shafter. With the regular radar crew off duty for the weekend, the main job of Private Joseph L. Lockard and Private George R. Elliott was to guard the set. Since Lockard knew how it worked, however, he and his buddy Elliott had been given the added responsibility of manning the set for several hours this morning. If they saw any blips on the scope, they were to report them by telephone to the information center back at Fort Shafter.

After they put the set into operation Lockard and Elliott saw almost nothing on the scope. But then, they hadn't

really expected to. They both knew they might just as well be in the sack sleeping or eating some early morning chow as spending their time sitting in front of a blank radarscope. That was the Army for you, though. Your life wasn't your own, even at four o'clock on a Sunday morning. But Lockard and Elliott were good soldiers. They had stood many other kinds of Army guard mount in the dim watches of the Pacific night, and they knew that this one, like all of the others, must sooner or later come to an end. They'd just have to sweat it out. Meanwhile, they had a job to do and they would do it. They continued to watch the scope for nonexistent blips.

Back at Fort Shafter's information center the enlisted men in the plotting crew also went on duty at four a.m. Their watch, like that of Lockard and Elliott manning the radar set, was to last until seven a.m. When the plotting crew went on duty they were joined by Lieutenant Kermit A. Tyler.

Tyler was a young fighter pilot. He had no specially assigned duty on this particular morning except to observe how the radar plane-tracking operation worked. He had heard that a flight of B-17 bombers was due to arrive from the United States today. The Navy also had its carriers out, and they might be sending up some planes. Tyler wondered if the two men at the mobile radar installation would spot the B-17's or the Navy fighters and report them back here to the information center so their location could be indicated on the big plotting board. But even if planes were spotted there was actually no one to whom the lieutenant could report such information. The entire radar set-up was on a practice basis, and its operation was almost a complete mystery to most service men at this time.

Lockard and Elliott at the radar set reported very little air activity. The hours dragged by. Finally, after what

Staff Sergeant Joseph L. Lockard wearing the Distinguished Service Medal. He reported the approach of unidentified planes to Hawaii on Sunday morning, December 7, 1941. (U.S. Army Photo)

seemed like days, seven o'clock arrived and the plotting crew went off duty. Lieutenant Tyler began to think about breakfast. Just then the telephone rang. It was Private Elliott reporting that he and Lockard had picked up something on the radarscope.

Lockard and Elliott had not shut down the set at seven o'clock. Their relief had not arrived so they dutifully continued to watch for blips. While Elliott was on the scope an enormous blip appeared.

"Hey, Joe, look at this!" he called excitedly.

Lockard looked. He had never seen such a large signal before.

"The set must be busted," he said. But a quick check proved that the set was in perfect working order. And the huge blip remained.

"What do you think it is?" Elliott asked.

"Planes," Lockard said. "A flock of 'em — fifty, sixty, maybe more. They're about a hundred and forty miles out."

"Shouldn't we call Shafter?" Elliott asked.

"Sure," Lockard said. "Go ahead. I'll stay on the set."

Lieutenant Tyler was puzzled but unalarmed by Elliott's report. If the two soldiers on the radar set said they had spotted some planes, he would have to take their word for it since they were at least partially familiar with the operation and he was just an observer trying to learn how it worked. He could not, of course, know what planes they had spotted. They could be off the Navy carriers. Or maybe they were the B-17's from the States.

"Don't worry about it," Lieutenant Tyler said. "Forget it."

But Lockard and Elliott continued to watch the radar image. It seemed to grow and grow. In a matter of minutes now it would become not merely an image but real airplanes, enemy airplanes, Japanese fighters and bombers bent on their deadly mission of attack on Pearl Harbor and its nearby airfields.

* * *

At Bellows Field, not far from Pearl Harbor, a twenty-two-year-old United States Army Air Force corporal had awakened early on this fateful Sunday morning. Harold Kolom and several of his squadron buddies were planning to go into Honolulu for the day. When Corporal Kolom had shaved, dressed, and eaten breakfast his friends still weren't ready to go, so he decided to write a letter to his girl, Shirley Dubow, back home in Chicago.

He went outside the tent and sat down near one of the squadron's planes. It was a calm and peaceful morning with fleecy white clouds floating lazily in the tropical skies. Corporal Kolom started to write his letter.

> *"Dearest Shirley,"* he wrote. *"The best thing that happened to me yesterday was my getting your letter. So glad to hear from you again and find you well and in good spirits. How are you, Shir? Trust and pray you are feeling much better now and always. Too bad about your having to give up the job but don't you fret about it, there are many many more and better ones for you. Please write me soon and let me know how you feel — I am worried over you. Please take care of yourself, keep well and Happy always!*
>
> *"Everything here is . . ."*

Corporal Kolom frowned in irritation as he heard someone shout, "Hey, that's a Jap plane!"

Just some hot Navy pilot buzzing the field, Kolom thought. They were always doing that.

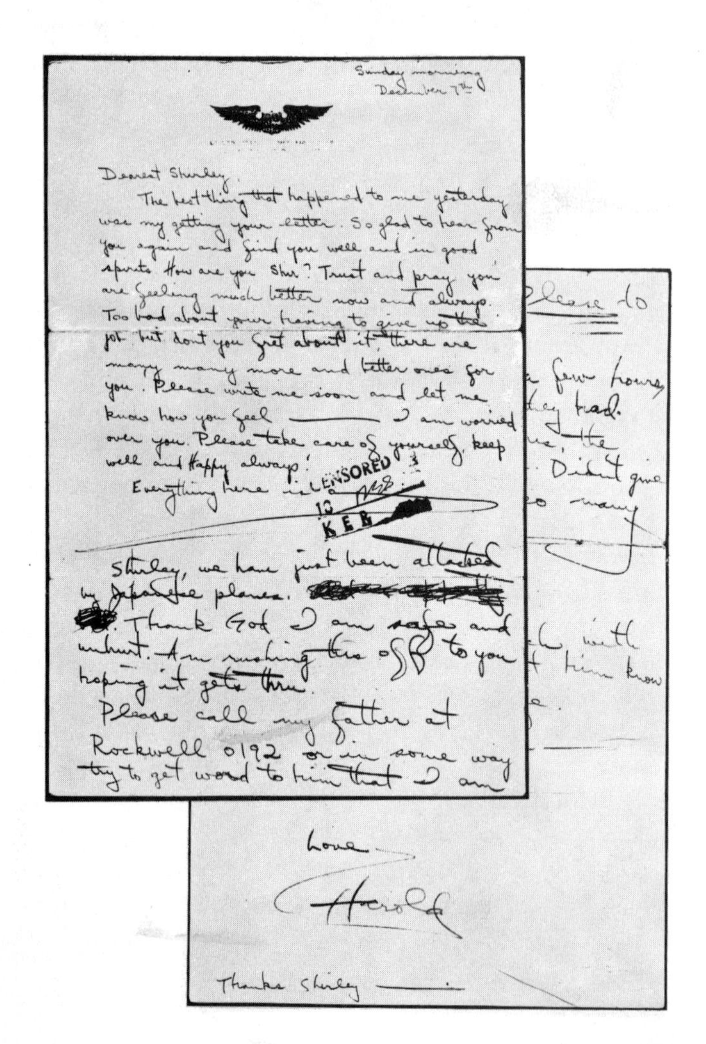
Sunday morning
December 7th

Dearest Shirley,

The best thing that happened to me yesterday was my getting your letter. So glad to hear from you again and find you well and in good spirits. How are you Shir? Trust and pray you are feeling much better now and always. Too bad about your having to give up the job but don't you fret about it, there are many many more and better ones for you. Please write me soon and let me know how you feel —— I am worried over you. Please take care of yourself, keep well and happy always!

Everything here is

CENSORED
13
KEB

Shirley, we have just been attacked by Japanese planes. Thank God I am safe and unhurt. Am rushing this off to you hoping it gets thru.

Please call my father at Rockwell 0192 or in some way try to get word to him that I am

Love —
Harold

Thanks Shirley ——

Army Air Force Corporal Harold Kolom was at Bellows Field, Hawaii, writing this letter to his girl, Shirley Dubow, on Sunday morning, December 7, 1941, when the Japanese struck Pearl Harbor and its nearby airfields. Kolom lived through the raid and was later returned to the United States to take flight training. He and Shirley were married in 1943. Shortly afterwards Kolom was the only one of eight men to survive a training accident. Today he and Shirley live in Chicago with their two daughters, Lois and Dale. (Courtesy Harold Kolom)

"You can see the 'meat ball' insignia on its wings!" Kolom heard someone else shout. "It must be a Zero!"

But what would a Japanese plane be doing flying toward a restricted area like Pearl Harbor?

Kolom had no further time to puzzle over the matter. The red air raid alert had sounded. He tossed down his letter and hurried to help some of the other members of the ground crew get the squadron's P-40 fighters and A-20 attack bombers ready for flight.

A moment later a B-17 came roaring in for a landing. It was one of the bombers that Lieutenant Tyler at Fort Shafter had heard would be arriving from the United States this morning. But what was a B-17 doing trying to land at Bellows Field? Corporal Kolom wondered. The big bombers were supposed to land at Hickam Field. Later he learned that the unarmed B-17 had tried to land at Hickam, which was right next to Pearl Harbor, but it had been attacked by Jap fighters. The pilot had tried to escape the attack by landing here at Bellows Field. Now, however, as it touched down for a landing the murderous Zeros were still on its tail. The Jap planes not only poured round after round of machine-gun fire into the helpless Flying Fortress but also raked the P-40's and A-20's lined up on the nearby runways.

Corporal Kolom saw several pilots climb into their planes and try to take off. Before they could clear the runways, they were destroyed by the low-flying Zeros. Corporal Kolom made a valiant effort to rescue one pilot from his burning plane, but he was already dead. Nearby, other flyers fought to get their planes airborne but were almost immediately hit by the strafing Japs. One pilot did manage to take off, but a few moments later he was shot down in the sea.

The raid seemed to go on and on. Zero after Zero came

One of the first photographs taken of the bombing of Hickam Field, Hawaii, December, 7 1941. Planes are B-17 Flying Fortress bombers.

streaking in just a few yards off the ground, machine guns hammering out death and destruction.

And then, as quickly as it had started, the attack on Bellows Field ended. When it was over, Corporal Kolom found the letter he had been writing and added a hasty last few lines. They read:

> *"Shirley, we have just been attacked by Japanese planes. Thank God I am safe and unhurt. Am rushing this off to you hoping it gets thru. Please call my father . . . or in some way try to get word to him that I am safe and unhurt. They attacked us for a few hours and shot at us with everything they had. They didn't give us a chance. They killed so many."*

Corporal Kolom wrote the postscript in something of a daze, not knowing if he would ever get to mail the letter or if it would ever reach Chicago. There was no doubt in his mind, or anybody else's, about what had happened. This had been no air raid drill but the real thing — a sneak Japanese attack. An invasion might follow at any minute. If so, Kolom expected to die. He signed the letter, *"Love, Harold,"* and as he wrote the words to Shirley he felt that they might be the last words he would ever write.

Corporal Kolom and the rest of the men of the Forty-fourth Pursuit Squadron at Bellows Field knew they had been dealt a terrible blow by the Japanese. They did not immediately realize, however, the full extent of the attack. Hours later they learned that the main target of the Japanese was the United States Pacific fleet lying peacefully at anchor in Pearl Harbor.

* * *

At 7:55 a.m. the first wave of Japanese planes came boil-

A wrecked fighter plane at Bellows Field, Hawaii, where Corporal Harold Kolom was writing the letter to his girl when the Japanese raid began. (U.S. Army Photo)

ing out of the sun to hit the ninety-six ships at Pearl Harbor, including the seven majestic battleships anchored side by side in "Battleship Row." An eighth battleship, the *Pennsylvania,* was in drydock undergoing repairs. Torpedo bombers skimmed in just a few feet above the water to launch their death-dealing torpedoes. Dive bombers dropped deadly armor-piercing shells that exploded deep below the battleships' decks.

The *Oklahoma* was hit by several torpedoes and within minutes had rolled completely over in the water. Of the 1,354 men on board, 415 were killed. The *Maryland* was more fortunate, getting hit by only a pair of bombs and losing several men. The *West Virginia* was struck by half a dozen torpedoes and several bombs. These killed more than 100 men of the 1,500 on board. The *Tennessee* was hit by several bombs that killed five men. The *California* soon began to sink after being struck by a pair of torpedoes that opened enormous holes in her side.

Searing, almost unbelievable tragedy struck the *Arizona.* Within minutes after the Japanese attack began, more than 1,100 of her 1,400 officers and men were killed when the battleship blew up after being hit by a series of bombs and torpedoes.

A rare display of courage took place on board the *Nevada.* Shortly before the attack began, the ship's color guard had started to raise the morning colors. As part of this ceremony the band was playing "The Star Spangled Banner" just as the first wave of Jap fighter planes strafed the battleship's deck. Not a man broke ranks until the playing of the national anthem was completed. A torpedo also hit the *Nevada.* Fifty of her officers and crew were killed.

The first Japanese attack lasted about half an hour. At 8:40 a.m. a second wave roared in. By now, anti-aircraft gunners were able to go into action with their guns and

The U.S.S. Shaw exploding during the Japanese raid on December 7, 1941. (U.S. Army Photo)

Wreckage of the naval air station at Pearl Harbor.

the Japs suffered a few losses. However, of the 353 Jap planes that took part in the raid only nine fighters and twenty bombers were shot down, with a loss of some fifty-five men.

The United States suffered tragic losses. Some eighteen major ships—destroyers, cruisers, and battleships—were sunk or seriously damaged. More than 2,000 Navy officers and men were killed and more than 700 wounded. This was three times as many men as the Navy had lost in the Spanish-American War and World War I combined.

The Army and Marines lost 327 killed and 433 wounded. In addition, the Japs had destroyed about half the military airplanes at six airfields on the island of Oahu. Most of these planes were destroyed on the ground. The Army Air Force lost more than a third of some 230 planes, and many fighters and bombers that weren't destroyed were severely damaged. The Navy and Marines lost three-quarters of their 150 planes.

In less than two hours the Japanese had dealt the United States the single most staggering blow in its military history. The Japanese did not declare war on the United States until several hours after their surprise attack. The next day the United States Congress declared that a state of war had existed since December 7, "a date," President Franklin D. Roosevelt said, "which will live in infamy."

* * *

The man who had first had the idea for a carrier-borne airplane strike against the United States Pacific fleet at Pearl Harbor was Japanese Admiral Isoroku Yamamoto. He had suggested it early in 1941. By midsummer a few Japanese pilots had been told about the plan. Actual flight training from the decks of Japanese airplane carriers did not begin, however, until that autumn.

Wrecked planes at Wheeler Field, Hawaii, after the Pearl Harbor raid. (U.S. Army Photo)

The Pearl Harbor raid was only one part of a master plan to conquer the whole of southeast Asia. Knocking out the heart of the Pacific fleet would keep it from interfering with Japan's other goals. These included the conquest of French Indochina, the Dutch East Indies, British Malaya, Thailand, and the Philippine Islands. If these plans succeeded, the Japanese later intended to conquer China.

Right up until the moment of the surprise raid, two Japanese ambassadors, Saburo Kurusu and Kichisaburo Nomura, were carrying on negotiations in Washington with United States Secretary of State Cordell Hull. Hull had been suspicious of Japanese diplomats for some little time. He once described them as being "as crooked as a basket full of fishhooks."

Hull and other Washington officials had good reasons for suspecting a Japanese act of war. Some months before December 7, 1941, the United States had succeeded in breaking the Japanese Purple code, the code used to send all major diplomatic messages. The operation of decoding Japanese messages was called "Magic." Thus long before the war began, Magic made it possible for high officials in Washington to know the details of all the top-secret communications that were being sent back and forth between Tokyo and Japan's two chief diplomats in the United States.

After the attack on Pearl Harbor, it seemed clear that these messages had indicated that such an attack was about to take place. Later investigations, however, failed to prove this fact. It was true that General Walter C. Short and Admiral Husband E. Kimmel, the top ranking Army and Navy officers at Pearl Harbor, were told on November 27 that there might be "hostile action at any minute," and the Navy sent a message saying, "This is to be considered a war warning." However, although everyone was expecting war to break out soon, no one in Washington or Hawaii expected it to break out at Pearl Harbor. Nevertheless, General Short and Admiral Kimmel were later removed from their commands.

One of the messages decoded by Magic from Tokyo to the Japanese ambassadors in Washington said that if war between the United States and Japan seemed certain the Japanese shortwave radio would broadcast the phrase "Higashi no kazeame." Translated, this meant "East wind, rain." This was to be the signal for the Japanese ambassadors to destroy all of their secret papers. United States intelligence officers kept listening for these words to be broadcast but, as far as is known today, they never were.

Fortunately, on the morning of the attack the United States Navy aircraft carriers *Enterprise* and *Lexington* were at sea carrying fighter planes to Wake and Midway islands. Had these carriers been at Pearl Harbor on the morning of December 7 they, too, would probably have been destroyed and the United States might never have recovered from the blow.

The Pearl Harbor attack was without question a disaster for the United States. It did, however, unite the nation as nothing else could have. Although World War II had been going on in Europe since September 1939, there was much anti-war feeling in the United States. A strong isolationist party had kept the United States from taking part in the actual fighting despite the fact that freedom's light was in danger of being put out by Adolf Hitler's Nazi Germany. The German war machine had all but taken over the continent. Russia was on the defensive in Eastern Europe. England alone remained a bastion of freedom in Western Europe, and it was struggling against overwhelming odds to keep from being defeated. After December 7, 1941, there was only one aim on the part of all

Americans: to win the war. "Remember Pearl Harbor!" became a defiant battle cry that rallied all Americans to the nation's cause.

On December 8, after the United States declared that a state of war had existed against Japan since the previous day, Great Britain also declared war on Japan. China then declared war against the Axis powers (Germany,Italy, and Japan). Germany and Italy declared war on the United States on December 11, and the United States Congress voted for war declarations in return. By January 1, 1942, some twenty-six nations were at war with the Axis powers.

Two

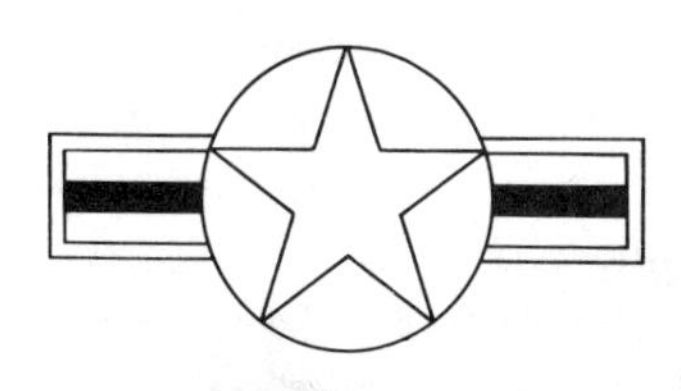

"Peace in Our Time"

The American doughboys who fought in World War I thought they were fighting a war to end all wars. They believed President Woodrow Wilson when he said a victory by the Allied nations over Kaiser Wilhelm's Germany would "make the world safe for democracy." Wilson himself believed this. However, the fighting had scarcely ended on the Western Front with the signing of the Armistice on November 11, 1918, before the seeds of the Second World War were being sown.

The treaty that officially ended World War I was called the Treaty of Versailles. Germany at first objected to its terms, claiming they were too harsh and not in keeping with President Wilson's pledge of peace without revenge. After some slight changes were made in the treaty, German officials signed it on June 28, 1919. The treaty was ratified by all of the Allied nations — with one exception, the United States. The reason the United States would not do so was that many Americans did not want the country to join the League of Nations.

The League of Nations had been President Wilson's idea, a part of his fourteen-point program for a better world. The last of Wilson's Fourteen Points suggested that "a general association of nations be formed to guarantee political independence and territorial integrity to all countries, large or small." Wilson believed that such an organization would enable all of the nations of the world to get along together in peace and harmony by settling their disagreements over a conference table instead of going to war over them. At Wilson's insistence, the constitution (called the Covenant) for the League of Nations was written into the Treaty of Versailles.

In an effort to persuade Americans that the United States should join the League, Wilson toured the nation in the fall of 1919 making speeches in defense of his idealistic plan. During the month of September he traveled some 8,000 miles and gave almost forty hour-long speeches warning that if America rejected the League there would be a second World War within twenty years.

Worn out from his efforts to establish a just and lasting peace, Wilson suffered a paralytic stroke at the end of the month and was taken back to the White House. There, from his sick bed, he continued to fight for the cause which he considered to be right. Despite the stricken President's dramatic efforts, the United States Senate twice refused to ratify the Versailles Treaty.

In the national election of 1920 Wilson received the final blow to his hopes that the United States might yet join the League of Nations. The Democrats favored the League and the Republicans opposed it. The Democratic candidate for President, James M. Cox, was overwhelmingly defeated by Republican Warren G. Harding. It was not until 1921 that the United States finally signed separate peace treaties with Austria and Germany.

Wilson died in 1924. His prediction regarding the start of World War II came true almost to the day.

In addition to establishing the League of Nations, the Treaty of Versailles disarmed Germany, changed its boundaries, and made provision for a committee (called a reparations commission) to decide how much the defeated nation was to pay for starting the war. Germany lost much of its former territory in Europe, as well as all of its overseas colonies. The reparations commission finally decided that Germany should pay the Allies more than thirty billion dollars in money and goods.

It was not long before Germany stopped making these reparations payments. Several plans were suggested for making the payments easier, but finally they were stopped altogether. During the early 1920's there was an economic inflation in Germany. The nation's money became worthless, and financial ruin was widespread.

In the United States the 1920's was an era of economic boom and prosperity. Turning their backs on Europe's problems, the American people were all in favor of Warren Harding's election promise of a return to "normalcy." When Harding died in office in 1923, Vice President Calvin Coolidge moved into the White House. Coolidge was so popular and the nation was so prosperous that he was returned to office as President in the election of 1924. (His inaugural ceremonies were the first to be broadcast by radio.) Coolidge firmly believed in few, if any, government controls on American business and industry. This "hands off" policy met with much favor among the people who were tired of wartime government controls and restrictions. "The business of America is business," Coolidge declared as he loosened the reins on all areas of the nation's economy. His words seemed to stand for a wild, free-spending era the like of which the nation had never seen.

Investing money in stocks — "playing the market" — became a national craze. Every day the price of stocks rose higher and higher on the New York market. A person buying a stock one day almost always found on the following day that the stock was worth more than he had originally paid for it. Thus, many people who gambled in the stock market saw themselves making what seemed to be huge profits. Since most people who sold their stocks turned right around and bought more, much of the money they seemed to be making they never actually received. Their profits were "paper profits." Many people also borrowed money to buy stocks "on margin." The upward spiral of the market looked as if it would never end, however, and everyone in America began to dream of becoming rich without having to work for the money. There was also a great boom in the building of new homes and other construction. Employment and wages reached all-time highs.

With more leisure time as well as money, everyone everywhere in the nation became keenly interested in recreation. Sports became big business as millions of fans watched "Babe" Ruth hit home runs, "Red" Grange score touchdowns, and Gene Tunney win the world's heavyweight boxing title from Jack Dempsey. In 1921 Ruth hit fifty-nine home runs, and in 1927 he hit sixty. As a result of the great interest "The Babe" created in baseball, World Series receipts each fall were more than a million dollars. In 1927 some thirty million fans paid more than fifty million dollars to watch football games. The Dempsey-Tunney fight the same year had gate receipts of more than two and a half million dollars. The 1920's were truly a Golden Era of sports.

The 1920's were also called the "Jazz Age," after the popular style of music of the times. Dancing was very popular, particularly one dance called the "Charleston." The decade also introduced the female "flapper." Women were now able to vote, following the passage of the Nineteenth Amendment, and for the first time they began to take part in many activities as equals alongside men. They also began to express their newborn independence in other ways. Having traditionally worn their hair long, they now cut it short in "boyish bobs." Dresses which had been ankle-length were shortened. In all walks of life in this period of frantic postwar prosperity, an attitude of gay, reckless freedom seemed abroad in the land.

There was, however, one new restriction in the United States. This was brought about by the Eighteenth Amendment to the Constitution, the so-called "National Prohibition Amendment," which prohibited the manufacture and sale of alcoholic beverages. The Federal government had great trouble enforcing this law after it went into effect in 1920.

Much of the disregard for the prohibition law as well as the general change in customs and manners could be traced directly to the war. Americans had entered World War I as innocent idealists. They had felt they were taking part in a great crusade for freedom. The wholesale killing of men on the Western Front and the quarrels at the peace table afterwards brought bitter disillusionment. People felt their ideals and their traditions had been betrayed. Now they turned away from them. Many people began to say that America should never have entered the war in the first place, and they were determined the nation should never enter another foreign conflict. Out of these attitudes of isolationism and pacifism, which people of other countries shared, grew a widespread belief in the possibility of doing away with war by worldwide disarmament.

International disarmament conferences were held in

Washington in 1921 and 1922. At these meetings France, Italy, Japan, England, and the United States agreed to limit the size of their navies. As a result of this agreement the United States destroyed twenty-eight battleships and six cruisers. The other nations did not destroy any of their war ships; they simply agreed not to build any new ones.

None of the nations could agree on limiting the size of their armies. A later conference called by the League of Nations at Geneva ended in complete disagreement. Germany was already threatening to re-arm despite the Versailles Treaty restrictions, and none of the other nations of Europe felt safe in the face of such a threat.

Some efforts for peace seemed more successful. The major nations of Europe signed the Locarno Pact to guarantee peace in Europe in 1925. In 1928 the Kellogg-Briand Pact of Paris condemning war was signed by all of the world's major powers.

Then, in 1929, a worldwide economic depression began. The unrest it brought seemed to stir up all of the old territorial problems in Europe and the Far East.

In the United States, Republican Herbert Hoover had been elected President at the peak of the economic boom in 1928. When he took office in 1929 he said that he thought America was on the verge of completely doing away with poverty. Like Harding and Coolidge, Hoover did not believe in government controls on business. Instead, he said, he believed in "rugged individualism" on the part of businessmen.

In the autumn of 1929 there was a severe drop in prices in the stock market. People who had thought the rise in stock prices would continue forever now learned a bitter truth: prices could go down just as fast as they went up. Fortunes were lost in a matter of hours. Life savings disappeared overnight as banks were forced to shut their doors. Soon a business decline set in throughout the country. Prices on all goods dropped. Unemployment increased as the wheels of industry all but ground to a halt. The farmers had been experiencing a depression long before the rest of the country. Now their situation became truly desperate. In the towns and cities across the land "bread-lines" — long lines of unemployed men seeking food from soup kitchens — became a familiar sight. World War I veterans sold pencils and apples on street corners.

Hoover, however, believed the depression was only a temporary thing.

"Prosperity is just around the corner," the President insisted.

During the depths of the depression, in 1931, the United States House of Representatives passed a bill authorizing a cash bonus for the veterans of World War I. The Senate defeated the measure. A "bonus army" of veterans then gathered and marched on Washington to demand that the Senate pass the bill. The Senate, backed by President Hoover, still refused to approve the measure, and the President went even further. He ordered Federal troops to disband the bonus army and drive its members out of Washington.

While the United States was concerned with its own economic problems, several events were taking place in the Far East and Europe that were actually steps along the road to the Second World War. Italy, Japan, and Germany claimed they were "have not" nations. They felt they had neither the territory nor the natural resources that other nations had. In time they formed the "Berlin-Rome-Tokyo Axis" to press home their claims for more land.

Japan made its first move to get more territory in 1931. It invaded Manchuria. The following year it invaded China. China called upon the League of Nations to take action against Japan, but the League did little about it. The United States said it would refuse to recognize any territory that the Japanese gained by conquest. Japan withdrew its troops from China for a time, but fighting flared up again in 1937.

In 1935 Benito Mussolini, Italy's dictator, sent troops into Ethiopia. Ethiopia's Emperor Haile Selassie turned to the League for help, but again little help was given. The Ethiopian soldiers, equipped only with spears and other primitive weapons, were slaughtered by Italy's mechanized armed forces. Later Italy also took over Albania.

* * *

Meanwhile there had come to power in Germany a little man with a comic mustache. His original family name was equally comical, Schicklgruber. This strange little man, who was called Adolf Hitler after his father changed the family name, was first thought of as a joke by other European leaders. Before long, however, he was to cause a reign of terror such as Europe had not seen since the Dark Ages.

Adolf Hitler was born on April 20, 1889, at Braunau, Austria. As a boy he wanted to become an artist. Lazy and untalented, he had little success as an art student. For some years he drifted from one job to another—common laborer, carpenter, and painter of water color postcards. When World War I started in 1914, Hitler enlisted in the German infantry. He fought in several battles, was gassed, wounded, decorated, and promoted to corporal. At the end of the war he would not believe that Germany had been defeated. Instead, he insisted the nation had been "sold out, stabbed in the back by the Jews and Communists." He regarded the Versailles Treaty as an insult to the German people.

In 1919 he joined the German Workers' Party, a group dedicated to creating a new and all-powerful German state. Hitler soon became a leader of this organization, changing its name to the National Socialist German Workers' (*Nazi*) Party. He made many violent speeches against the Jews and Communists, whom he blamed for Germany's postwar depression. The Nazis adopted the swastika as their party emblem and greeted one another with a raised arm salute and the words "Heil, Hitler!"

In 1923 Hitler was sent to jail for trying to overthrow the German government. While in jail he wrote a book called *Mein Kampf* (My Struggle), in which he outlined his political program and ideas for creating a strong Germany. Released from jail in 1924, Hitler set about putting his political ideas to work. It was not until the worldwide economic depression started in 1929, however, that he and his Nazi Party gained recognition. Then the Germans began to turn to him as a savior. They believed his promises that if he were in power he would end unemployment, re-arm the nation to save it from the Communists and other foreign enemies, and regain Germany's position as a leading world power.

In 1933 he became Chancellor of Germany. From then on he moved relentlessly along the road to war. He quickly became the nation's complete dictator, outlawing rival political parties and putting his opponents in jail. In open defiance of the Versailles Treaty he began to re-arm Germany. He created a new army and air force and increased the size of the navy. His most serious threats to peace were his demands for additional territory in Europe.

* * *

Although all of the American people continued to have a sincere desire for a lasting peace, many of them now began to realize they could not achieve peace by ignoring the problems of the rest of the world. In 1932 they elected a new President who believed that the United States should play a leading role in world affairs, Franklin D. Roosevelt.

Roosevelt had served as Assistant Secretary of the Navy under President Wilson during World War I. After the war he had worked tirelessly to get the United States to join the League of Nations. In 1920 he had been nominated by the Democrats as the candidate for Vice President to run for election with Presidential nominee James Cox. Although Cox and Roosevelt were defeated by Harding and Coolidge, young Roosevelt was still determined to enter the White House one day.

His dreams of leading the nation were almost destroyed in 1921 when he was stricken with infantile paralysis. The attack left him permanently crippled in body but not in spirit. By 1924 he was back in the thick of politics. In 1928 he was elected Governor of New York. He was re-elected in 1930.

With some twelve million men out of work in the United States in 1932 and the nation's economy all but paralyzed, the people were eager for new leadership. Democratic Presidential nominee Franklin Roosevelt promised them a "New Deal." They elected him by an overwhelming majority.

Most of the new President's reforms dealt with the national economy. He believed that the government should take a strong, active part in business. His New Deal measures provided immediate financial relief for the needy, gave special aid to the farmers, and introduced new controls over banking and industry. One of his most far-reaching plans was a method for providing unemployment and old age insurance (Social Security). Although many businessmen were opposed to Roosevelt because they regarded his New Deal measures as dangerously radical, he was re-elected in 1936.

During this same year a civil war broke out in Spain

which was to be a training ground for many of the men and a testing ground for much of the equipment later used in World War II. Italy and Germany sent their Fascist and Nazi troops to aid Francisco Franco's Nationalists in their rebellion against the government. Russian soldiers fought on the side of the Spanish Loyalists. A number of young Americans also fought on the Loyalist side as volunteer members of the International Brigade. Many of the 2,800 Americans who took part in this war were idealistic students who felt they were fighting against the spirit of dictatorship which threatened Europe. They served in the Abraham Lincoln and George Washington Battalions. About 900 of them were killed. In 1939 Franco's forces overthrew the Spanish government and the rebel leader was installed as Spain's dictator.

Not all Americans, however, felt that their freedom was at stake as the forces of aggression continued their warlike march. In 1937 Japanese airplanes sank the United States gunboat *Panay* and several tankers in the Yangtze River in China, killing several American citizens. The United States promptly protested and the American people seemed eager to accept the Japanese apology.

The tide of isolationism continued to run strong in Europe as well as in America, even in the face of open acts of aggression by Adolf Hitler's Nazi Germany. The Versailles Treaty had stated there should be no military troops in the Rhineland, between the Rhine River and France. However, early in 1936 Hitler sent his troops into this demilitarized zone. When he met no opposition in this violation of the Treaty, Hitler decided to unite Austria and Germany, which had also been forbidden. The Nazis assassinated Austria's Chancellor Engelbert Dollfuss and took over his country in 1938. No nation made a serious effort to stop these moves.

The little corporal with the Charlie Chaplin mustache was not regarded as a comical figure now. In fact, Allied leaders began to call him a madman who was threatening the peace of the world.

Hitler continued his warlike moves. There were some three and a half million "Germans" living in Czechoslovakia. These people should be under German rule, the Nazi leader said. He also added, "This is my last territorial demand in Europe."

With Europe now on the brink of war, Great Britain's Prime Minister Neville Chamberlain and France's Premier Edouard Daladier flew to Munich to meet with Hitler. Without consulting the Czech government, Chamberlain and Daladier gave in to Hitler's demands for Czech territory.

Chamberlain flew back to London and declared the Munich agreement meant "peace with honor. I believe it is peace in our time." His words were greeted with wild enthusiasm except by one British statesman, who let out a wounded lion's roar.

"We have sustained a total defeat!" Winston Churchill said. He added to Chamberlain, "You chose dishonor, and you will have war!"

This attempted appeasement failed to satisfy Hitler. He was soon making threatening demands upon Poland. He wanted a piece of Polish land that he promised would be his "last territorial claim."

Now, however, both France and England took a firm stand. Chamberlain and Daladier said that their nations would go to war if Poland were attacked. Hitler either did not believe them or else did not care if they were speaking the truth.

But there was one thing the Nazi leader did not want, to fight a war on two fronts — against England, France, and the other Allies on the west and Russia on the east. He had seen the disaster this caused Germany in World War I, and he did not intend to make the same mistake. Late in August 1939 Hitler signed a pact with Russia in which Russia agreed to remain neutral if Germany went to war.

The announcement of the German-Soviet agreement fell like a bombshell among the Allied leaders. Russia had suffered severely at the hands of Germany in World War I, going down to defeat in March 1918. In 1917, during the war, there had been a revolution in Russia. This revolution was led by Nikolai Lenin. The form of government that Lenin and his followers set up was called Communism. Communism was supposed to create a state controlled by all of the people ("workers"). In reality it became the worst kind of dictatorship. The first Communist dictator in the Union of Soviet Socialist Republics was Lenin. Following his death, Joseph Stalin became the country's iron-fisted ruler.

One of the beliefs of the Communists was that their form of government should be forced upon every country of the world. Hitler had fought against the Communists who had tried to get control of the German government. Now he had made peace with the very people whom he claimed he despised.

Despite England's and France's grim warning, Hitler now turned his full attention upon Poland. On the bleak, gray dawn of September 1, 1939, motorized columns of Nazi troops roared into Poland. World War II had begun. England and France declared war on Germany on September 3. Within a few days Australia, Canada, India, New Zealand, and South Africa had entered the conflict at England's side. The United States announced that it would remain neutral.

Three

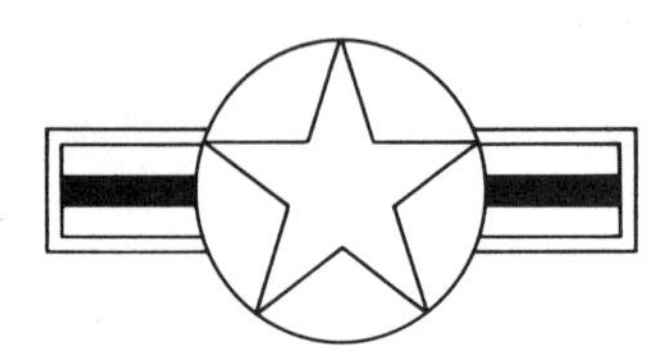

The War Before Pearl Harbor

Germany's conquest of Poland took just four weeks. The method of fighting used by the Germans was a new one. It was called *blitzkrieg* — "lightning war." The Nazi Air Force, the *Luftwaffe,* led the attack, destroying the Polish Air Force before it could get off the ground. Fast-moving motorized columns of armored vehicles (*panzers*) quickly divided the Polish Army into small units. Parachute troops and regular infantry were then used to surround these units. Then fierce artillery bombardment and infantry attacks destroyed these islands of Polish resistance.

The *Luftwaffe* used terror tactics against Polish civilians. People fleeing the German invasion were machine-gunned from the air as they swarmed along roads and highways. *Stuka* dive bombers equipped with siren-like whistles came howling out of the skies to bomb towns and cities.

Warsaw was the last Polish city to fall. By mid-September Germany had crushed all resistance except the defensive forces surrounding the ancient capital. Then Russia invaded Poland from the east. Still Warsaw refused to surrender. Hour after hour, day after day, the Warsaw radio continued to broadcast the Polish national anthem. The song was heard not only in Europe but was rebroadcast to the United States. Finally, on September 27, the Warsaw radio went dead. On September 28, 1939, Poland was divided between Germany and Russia.

For more than seven months after the fall of Poland, there was very little fighting on land between Germany and the Allies, France and England. This period became known as the "bore war," "sitzkrieg," or "phony war." Between World War I and World War II the French, under the direction of French Minister of War André Maginot, had built a series of concrete and steel fortifications to defend themselves from German attack. The French armies now sat comfortably in the Maginot Line, believing they were safe from attack. Opposite the Maginot Line was the German West Wall or Siegfried Line, a series of similar fortifications where the Nazi armies sat and waited. The Germans set up a number of loudspeakers over which they broadcast daily messages to the French, telling them they were foolish to let the war continue. Hitler even offered to make peace with England and France if they would accept his conquest of Poland, but the offer was rejected.

The war at sea was quite active during the winter of 1939-40. Hitler believed his submarines and pocket battleships could blockade England and starve the nation into surrender. Britain's fleet reacted by blockading Germany. Much shipping was sunk by both sides.

The British fleet suffered a severe blow on October 14 when the battleship *Royal Oak* was sunk at anchor at Scapa

Flow, the Royal Navy's carefully guarded base north of Scotland. Some 800 men were trapped and drowned inside the *Royal Oak*. Credit for sinking the great ship was claimed by the German submarine U-47 and its commander, Lieutenant Gunther Prien. The victory caused great joy throughout Germany, and Hitler personally awarded Prien the Knight's Cross of the Iron Cross.

After the war, however, certain doubts were cast on Prien's story of the sinking, and it was thought the *Royal Oak* might have been sabotaged. Prien himself disappeared mysteriously during the war. The Germans said he died when the U-47 was sunk by the British warship *Wolverine,* but there were rumors that he died in a German concentration camp or in a prisoner-of-war camp in the United States.

On December 13 the German pocket battleship *Graf Spee* was attacked by three British cruisers off the coast of South America and driven into the harbor at Montevideo, Uruguay. Uruguay was a neutral nation and told Captain Hans Langsdorff of the *Graf Spee* that he could keep his ship in the harbor for repairs only until December 17. Newspapers in the United States headlined the dramatic situation, and radio news broadcasts gave hourly reports on the promised sea battle. Langsdorff did not want his ship interned by Uruguay. Neither did he want the British to have the satisfaction of sinking it. The British cruisers, joined now by other warships, lay in wait just outside the mouth of the Plata River. To avoid disgracing himself in the eyes of *Der Führer* (the leader), as Hitler was called, Langsdorff ordered the *Graf Spee* sunk and he committed suicide.

Meanwhile, the Russians were engaged in conquests of their own. They moved into the Baltic states of Estonia, Latvia, and Lithuania in the autumn of 1939. In November they attacked Finland. The Finns put up surprising resistance, battling the Russians fiercely under almost impossible combat conditions of deep snow and temperatures as low as thirty degrees below zero. By March 1940 the Russians had smashed their way through Finland's Mannerheim Line, which was similar to the Maginot and Siegfried Lines. It was named for Baron Carl von Mannerheim, commander of the Finnish Army, who later became Finland's President. The defeat by the Russians cost the Finns almost 17,000 square miles of territory as well as several important cities and harbors.

A month later the Germans occupied Denmark and Norway. In Norway they met with stiff resistance not only from the Norwegians but also from the British who sent forces to Narvik. In this attack the Nazis used a number of parachute troops, as they had in conquering Poland. They also used a "fifth column." (This term grew out of the Spanish Civil War, when General Emilio Mola attacked Madrid. Under his command were four columns of infantry. Inside Madrid he also had a number of spies working for him. "They are my fifth column," he said.)

The fifth column of Nazi sympathizers in Norway was led by an army officer named Vidkun Quisling. He and his followers did a good job of destroying the Norwegian defense effort. Norway fell early in June. The free world so despised Quisling that today his name appears in the dictionary as a synonym for traitor. Quisling was finally executed by a firing squad on October 23, 1945.

As the forces of aggression gradually took over Europe, many people in the enemy-occupied countries set up secret "underground" armies. In Norway and later in France when that nation fell to the Nazis, these civilian freedom fighters gave the enemy not a moment's peace. Risking their lives daily, they waylaid and killed German soldiers, blew up railways and bridges, poisoned food in military supply depots, and aided Allied flyers shot down over German-held territory to escape to England.

Out of this resistance movement grew the "V for Victory" symbol. No one knows where the symbol was first used. It seemed to spring up suddenly all over Europe. People began painting it on walls, chalking it on streets and sidewalks, and making the V sign with their fingers. Although no one knew where it came from, everybody knew "V for Victory" meant resistance to the Nazis.

The British made good use of the fact that in Morse code the letter V is three dots and a dash. Broadcasting to the occupied countries, a British announcer named Colonel Britton pointed out early in the war that the opening notes of Beethoven's Fifth Symphony sounded the dot, dot, dot, dash V of the Morse code. Throughout the rest of the war, when the British Broadcasting Company went on the air with its newscasts to the continent the Beethoven "V for Victory" music was used as an introductory theme.

People on the continent spread the sounds everywhere, tapping them out with pencils on their desk tops, or with the toes of their shoes like tap dancers. They whistled the notes or hummed them in restaurants and other public places. When Winston Churchill became Prime Minister of England on May 10, 1940, he adopted the "V for Victory" sign of two spread fingers, and he is often credited with having been the first person to think of the symbol.

Almost from the very moment he replaced Chamberlain as British Prime Minister, Churchill became one of the war's legendary figures. He had been out of political power during most of the years between the two World Wars. But he had been an outspoken foe of Hitler since the early 1930's, when the Nazi leader had made his first territorial demands in Europe. During World War I, Churchill had been First Lord of the Admiralty, and when World War

II began he was again named to that post. Churchill had always been popular with the men of the Royal Navy. When he returned to duty with them, a message went out to the entire fleet: "Winston is back!"

The Nazi successes and British failures in Norway — they were forced to evacuate Narvik — brought about Chamberlain's fall and Churchill's rise to power. Churchill promised the British people no miracles. He told them simply, "I have nothing to offer but blood, toil, tears, and sweat." It was the kind of message the British wanted to hear. They were eager to meet whatever challenge, to make whatever sacrifice was necessary. The challenge came almost immediately.

On the very same day that Churchill became Prime Minister, the phony war ended abruptly on the Franco-German border as the Nazi *Luftwaffe* and armies struck without warning against Belgium, Luxembourg, and the Netherlands. Luxembourg offered no resistance, and the Dutch were forced to surrender within a few days. Belgium managed to hold out for a few weeks, but on May 28 King Leopold surrendered the Belgium forces. The famed Maginot Line proved worthless. Instead of attacking it head-on, the Germans swung around its weak north flank and raced to the English Channel at Abbeville. Hard-driving Nazi armored columns divided the Allied lines, cutting off several hundred thousand soldiers of the northern armies from the rest of France. Most of the troops trapped in the pocket with their backs to the English Channel were members of the British Expeditionary Forces, who had begun landing in France on September 4, 1939. They were now threatened with destruction, and the loss of the B.E.F. would all but knock England out of the war.

Somehow, the B.E.F. and as many of the other Allied forces as possible had to be evacuated from the continent by sea. The prospects did not look good. Churchill, in fact, warned the members of the House of Commons that they would have to be prepared to receive bad news.

At the same time, orders went out from Admiral Bertram Ramsay at Dover to the Royal Navy to use every available ship in an attempt to get the B.E.F. off the beaches at Dunkirk. The B.E.F. under Field Marshal John Gort fought a remarkably skillful delaying action. As its defense lines gradually drew back, fighting off the Germans every step of the way, thousands of troops began to stream toward Dunkirk. Many of the British "Tommies" brought with them a number of stray dogs that had become their pets while they were in France, and one soldier even brought his French bride of a few weeks. Disguising her in a British uniform he was able to bring her safely to England.

At Dunkirk the B.E.F. and retreating French forces were met, not only by destroyers, minesweepers, and other warships, but also by civilian boats of all kinds and description. These included paddlewheel ferry boats that had been used in peacetime to take sightseers across the English Channel, tugs that were normally used to move cargo ships in the Thames River, fishing smacks, private sail and motor boats, as well as private yachts — an armada of almost anything that would float and carry a few men. Traditionally a seagoing nation, the British civilian population rallied to this challenge as courageously as did their Royal Navy, not only offering whatever boats they owned for the venture but also offering to sail these boats themselves and help rescue the besieged soldiers. Included among these rescue crews were a number of teenaged British Sea Scouts.

The rescue effort was called "Operation Dynamo." When it began, Churchill estimated that at best some 45,000 men might be brought off the beaches. When it was finished, Churchill — who had promised no miracles when he took office — was able to tell the British people that virtually the entire B.E.F. as well as a number of French troops had been saved. During the incredible nine days from May 26 through June 4, 1940, some 1,200 ships of all kinds rescued almost 350,000 men. Dunkirk proved to be one of the greatest military evacuations in history. Churchill cautioned the British people that "evacuations don't win wars." Nevertheless, Operation Dynamo was regarded as a victory over the Germans and caused great rejoicing throughout England.

The day after Operation Dynamo ended, the final phase of the Battle of France began. Within two weeks the Nazis had captured Paris; the French government moved to Tours and then Bordeaux. On June 10, Italy, hoping to get in on some of the spoils, declared war on England and France. On June 17, France's Marshal Henri Pétain, hero of World War I, asked for surrender terms.

Hitler took this opportunity to avenge Germany's defeat in World War I. He demanded that the armistice be signed at the same city, Compiègne, and in the same railroad car in which Marshal Ferdinand Foch had dictated the armistice terms to the German officials in 1918. The Franco-German peace terms were signed on June 22 and the Franco-Italian terms on June 24. The Germans occupied all of northern and western France, including Paris. The French Navy was a prize desired by both the Nazis and the British. Some ships that were at sea joined the British. A number that did not were bombarded by the Royal Navy at Oran, Algeria.

With the defeat of France, England now stood alone.

Hitler was certain that England would surrender after the fall of France. He even offered what he thought were generous peace terms. When his offer was ignored, Hitler issued an order on July 16 stating that plans should be made for the invasion of Great Britain. The code name "Sea Lion" was given to this operation.

For many years after the summer of 1940, there were rumors that the Germans had actually attempted an invasion of England and failed. There were stories about bodies of horribly burned German soldiers being washed up along the Channel coast in the south of England. These stories probably grew out of the fact that the British did build pipelines down to the edge of the English Channel through which oil could be pumped. The oil was to have been ignited in an effort to destroy any invasion attempt in a barrage of flame. The experiment was abandoned, however, as impractical.

It is true that on September 7 the code word "Cromwell" was issued to defensive forces throughout southern England. Some people thought "Cromwell" meant that the invasion was under way. This, however, was a false alarm. Operation Sea Lion was never actually launched, because the *Luftwaffe* was defeated by the Royal Air Force in the skies over England. Without command of the air, Hitler and his generals knew, an invasion of England was impossible.

Hermann Goering, commander of the *Luftwaffe,* told Hitler that his planes could smash the Royal Air Force in less than a month. On August 12, 1940, the *Luftwaffe* prepared to live up to its leader's boast. This was the start of an epic battle that lasted until October 31. It is now known as the Battle of Britain, and, like the first Battle of the Marne in World War I, it marked a turning point in the war.

The British fighter command under Air Chief Marshal Sir Hugh Dowding had two superb fighter aircraft — the Hurricane and the Spitfire. Each carried eight guns and each was powered by the Rolls-Royce Merlin engine. The

Spitfire became the more widely known of the two planes, but in the Battle of Britain the "Hurry" actually outnumbered the "Spit" two-to-one.

These two superb planes were manned by equally superb pilots. This handful of British boys, in their teens and early twenties, flew into battle as many as seven times a day for week after week against the countless waves of German fighters and bombers. They flew up from such fighter command fields as those at Biggin Hill and Hornchurch—young, laughing, valiant pilots who were sometimes called the "Brylcreem Boys" because they seemed to be more concerned about their hair being combed correctly than they were about being shot down by the *Luftwaffe*.

The R.A.F. was greatly aided by the chain of radar stations set up along the British coast, as well as inland. Radar, which had been perfected by British physicist Sir Robert Watson-Watt, detected the formations of German planes long before they arrived over England. The R.A.F. was also helped by the fact that it was fighting over its own territory. Thus, if a pilot were shot down, he could often parachute out of his disabled plane and live to fight another day.

The most severe fighting during the Battle of Britain took place on August 15, 1940. On this day the *Luftwaffe* sent over 1,790 planes, including 520 bombers and 1,270 fighters. The R.A.F. shot down seventy-six German planes and lost thirty-four of its own. The next day 1,720 German planes attacked England; the R.A.F. shot down forty-five of them with a loss of twenty-two. The next day the Germans lost seventy-one planes to the R.A.F.'s twenty-seven. This ratio of losses was crippling to the *Luftwaffe*, which finally gave up the series of daylight attacks. During the entire Battle of Britain, the R.A.F. destroyed 1,733 planes and lost 915.

Winston Churchill summed up Germany's first decisive

defeat with these words: "Never in the field of human conflict was so much owed by so many to so few."

England's devastation by the *Luftwaffe* did not end with the end of the Battle of Britain. German bombers continued to make night raids on English cities for months. London was bombed for eighty-two nights out of eighty-five in the fall of 1940. The *Luftwffe* then turned its fury on other English cities. The purpose of this *blitz* was to terrorize the British people into surrender. Not once, however, did they falter.

During this tragic period, President Roosevelt did everything in his power, short of entering the war, to help the besieged nation. In September he and Churchill worked out an arrangement whereby the British were given fifty United States World War I destroyers in return for ninety-nine-year leases on British naval and air bases in the Western Hemisphere.

In January 1941 the United States Congress began to consider a bill whose number reminded Americans of their own trial by fire during the American Revolution, the Lend-Lease bill, numbered "1776." It was passed by Congress in March. Lend-Lease permitted President Roosevelt to supply United States war materials to any nation whose defense was vital to the United States. Under this bill a steady stream of war materials flowed to Great Britain. Winston Churchill described Lend-Lease as "the most unselfish act in history."

At sea the Battle of the Atlantic grew hot in 1941. Actually the United States Navy was fighting an undeclared war against Germany as U.S. destroyers attacked German submarines trying to sink American merchantmen which were carrying Lend-Lease supplies to England. One of the most dramatic sea fights of the war took place in May when the German battleship *Bismarck* sank the Royal Navy's battleship *Hood*. The *Bismarck* was in turn sunk by the British cruiser *Dorsetshire* off the coast of France.

Despite the sympathy that most Americans felt for the British, the isolationist movement was still powerful in the United States. A law permitting the first American peacetime draft of men for military service had been passed on September 16, 1940. This Selective Service Law authorized keeping drafted men in the Army for just one year and did not permit sending them overseas.

Many draftees entered the Army reluctantly and were unenthusiastic about military training. In 1940 an incident took place near a Southern training camp that was typical of many Americans' reaction against peacetime conscription. A group of draftees riding in trucks passed a golf course on which two girls were playing golf. The draftees whistled at the girls and called out "Yoo-hoo!" An Army officer, General Ben Lear, was playing golf nearby. He ordered the trucks to stop and directed that the draftees make a long march to their camp. Newspapers headlined the story everywhere in the United States, and civilian reaction was violent against the general, who was sarcastically called Ben "Yoo-Hoo" Lear.

In 1941, less than four months before Pearl Harbor, Congress was urged by Army Chief of Staff George C. Marshall to extend the length of service for drafted men and to permit the sending of draftees overseas. By this time many of the peacetime draftees were threatening to leave the Army with or without permission when their required year of service was ended in October. The word "OHIO," standing for "over the hill in October," was painted on Army barracks in many training camps, and stories about the movement were printed in the press. Nevertheless, the Selective Service Extension Act was passed by Congress — but by the slim margin of a single vote — on August 12, 1941.

As had been true in the past, however, there was a small

General George C. Marshall. (U.S. Army Photo)

corps of dedicated United States Regular Army officers who held firmly to a belief in American preparedness. These professional Army officers were responsible for the full-scale maneuvers held in Louisiana in September 1941. Here some half a million men divided into two "armies" took part in the largest peacetime war games in the nation's history.

The lessons learned during these maneuvers were to prove of great value in the war years ahead. When they were over, a group of officers met at Camp Polk, Louisiana, to discuss the military mistakes that had been made. In newspaper photographs of this meeting one of the officers was mistakenly identified as "Lieutenant Colonel D. D. Ersenbeing." This little-known officer was actually Dwight D. Eisenhower, who would one day lead the successful assault on Hitler's European fortress.

Meanwhile, the entire picture of the war in Europe had changed. Hitler had given up his plans for invading and defeating England. He decided to break his nonaggression pact with Russia and conquer the whole of the European continent. Before dawn on June 22, 1941, Germany attacked Russia. Remembering the trouble that the Russians had had in defeating Finland, Hitler announced to the German people that the crack Nazi armies could defeat Russia in a few months.

As soon as Germany attacked Russia, Churchill wasted no time in claiming the Soviet Union as an ally. "Any man or state who fights against Nazidom will have our aid," he said. "Any man or state who marches with Hitler is our foe." The United States immediately began to send Lend-Lease military supplies to Russia.

Before the year was out, Germany had advanced to within twenty-five miles of Moscow. Here the Nazi troops were stopped by the Soviet armies and an opponent the Russians called "General Winter." The Russian winter brought temperatures of forty degrees below zero, and the Germans had not been issued winter clothing or winter lubricants for their vehicles.

Japan had also continued its aggressive moves in the Far East, and Japanese-American relations grew steadily worse. The United States had stopped selling scrap iron and steel to Japan late in 1940. In July 1941 all Japanese financial assets in the United States were seized by the government. Later an oil embargo and other similar economic measures (called sanctions) were used against Japan. The United States gave as much aid as possible to China's General Chiang Kai-shek, who was leading his people in a fierce but futile fight against the invading Japanese.

To protect its interests in the Pacific the United States, early in the war, had moved its Pacific fleet to Pearl Harbor from San Diego. This was thought to be a safe action and one that would prevent the Japanese from taking over such undefended areas as the oil-and-metals-rich Dutch East Indies and French Indochina.

But the Japanese were determined to go to war. In October 1941 General Hideki Tojo became Premier of Japan. It was the warlike Tojo who instructed the Japanese ambassadors, Nomura and Kurusu, to carry on the false peace negotiations with United States Secretary of State Cordell Hull.

On Sunday, December 7, 1941, Nomura and Kurusu asked to have a conference with Secretary Hull. A moment before meeting with the Japanese ambassadors, Hull was told by an aide about the attack on Pearl Harbor that was even then going on. Nevertheless, the Secretary of State had Nomura and Kurusu ushered into his office. They gave him a message from Tojo that was supposed to be a final reply to an earlier American plan for peace in the Pacific. The message had already been decoded by Operation

Magic, so Hull knew its contents. Nevertheless, he pretended to read it. It was filled with insults and lies and false accusations against the United States. In a voice that was hot with anger, Hull then told the two ambassadors what he thought of them, their government, and the message. Finally he said, "In all of my fifty years of public service I have never seen a document that was more crowded with falsehoods and distortions on a scale so huge that I never thought any government on this planet could utter them!"

Silently the two Japanese left the office.

England no longer stood alone. The United States had become her ally in the grim battle to save Western civilization.

* * *

The United States' entry into the war brought a distinct feeling of relief to many Americans. For months war had seemed inevitable. Not many persons, of course, had expected an attack by Japan. But almost everyone had assumed that sooner or later the United States would be forced to take part in the war in Europe.

It had not been easy to stand by while Hitler and his savage Nazis tried to turn the clock of civilization back to the Dark Ages. It was not only Hitler's conquest of free nations that disturbed the conscience of America. It was also the barbaric butchery with which he was attempting to wipe out whole populations. For years grim stories had been coming out of Europe about the dreaded Nazi concentration camps. As the war continued, the free world was to learn of the even more dreadful extermination camps where millions of innocent men, women, and children were murdered.

The Nazi concentration camp system was set up by Hermann Goering. The camps were first used as prisons for political opponents of the Nazis, but they were soon filled with Jews and other minority groups hated by Hitler. Many inmates had been imported from nations the Nazis had conquered, to be used as "slave laborers" on road gangs, in factories, and on construction crews.

Conditions in the camps were unbelievably bad. Many inmates died of starvation or exposure to severe weather conditions; many were crippled or killed by savage S.S. (*Schutzstaffeln*) guards. Prisoners were maimed or murdered in medical experiments in which they served as "guinea pigs."

The extermination camps were set up during the war by S.S. Chief Heinrich Himmler. Their main purpose was to kill off Jews and other "inferior races" so Hitler could establish a "master race." In such concentration and extermination camps as Auschwitz, Buchenwald, and Belsen some six million Jews died, or were put to death in gas chambers disguised as bath houses; their bodies were cremated.

The whole story of Nazi Germany's concentration and extermination camps was not learned until after the war. Enough of it was known in the war's early stages, however, to make the American people realize that Hitler and his Nazis were an evil to be destroyed. General Eisenhower was to call the war in Europe a "great Crusade." He did not use the term lightly.

Americans, however, had their first direct experience with savage barbarism in World War II not at the hands of the Germans but at the hands of the Japanese, at Bataan and Manila in the Philippines.

Four

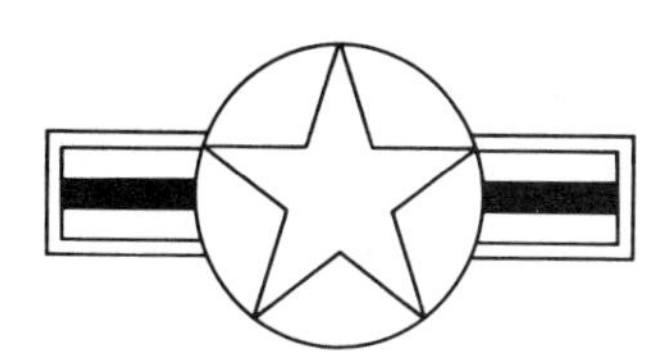

Defeat in The Pacific

The United States suffered a series of "Dunkirks" of its own during the winter of 1941-1942. These took place in the mid-Pacific and in the Philippines a short time after the Japanese struck at Pearl Harbor. Unlike the B.E.F. at Dunkirk in Europe, however, there were few troops rescued when the Japanese captured American island outposts in the Pacific and finally the Philippines.

Between Hawaii and the Philippines there were three key American islands — Midway, Wake, and Guam. To prevent the United States from using them as bases from which to mount an attack, the Japanese quickly took over Wake and Guam. They also tried to take over Midway, but here United States forces defeated two early invasion attempts.

Guam was unfortified and its 555 men were forced to

surrender to the invading Japanese early in December. Wake Island, whose small Navy and Marine garrison was led by Commander W. Scott Cunningham, put up a stout resistance. A number of civilian construction workers on Wake, who were building an air and submarine base, also helped in the fighting.

A few hours after they had received word that Pearl Harbor was being attacked, the Wake Island defenders were fighting off their first Japanese air raid. For the next two weeks there were air raids almost daily, and on December 11 an invasion was attempted but was successfully beaten off.

The eyes of everyone in America were now focused on this tiny strip of coral far out in the Pacific. It was reported that when the Navy headquarters at Pearl Harbor asked the men on Wake what they needed, this reply was received: "Send us more Japs!" But after the war both Commander Cunningham and Major James Devereux of the Marine defense battalion denied having sent such a report.

"If there was anything we did *not* need at Wake," Commander Cunningham said, "it was more Japs."

On December 23 Cunningham did send a message. It read, "Enemy on island. Issue in doubt." The issue was not long in doubt. No further word came from Wake. It, like Guam, had fallen, and the American flag would not fly over it again until late in 1945. Guam was recaptured in 1944.

The Japanese invasion of the Philippines began on December 10. On this same day Japanese planes sank the British battle-cruiser *Repulse* and the battleship *Prince of Wales,* which had been based with other ships of the Royal Navy at Singapore. Now it seemed that Singapore would fall, and the Philippines also appeared doomed.

General Douglas MacArthur was in command of the

General Douglas MacArthur. (U.S. Army Photo)

Philippines, where he and his family had been living when the war began. Under him were some 125,000 men. Actually, however, his trained, front-line troops amounted to no more than a few thousand U.S. Regular Army soldiers and Filipino scouts. These soldiers bore the brunt of the Japanese attack. The other troops were untrained.

The Philippine-based Army Air Force under General Lewis Brereton lost most of its planes in the Japanese air raids on Manila's Clark Field that began a few hours after the raid on Pearl Harbor. Naval defenses had also been destroyed when the Japanese bombers hit the Cavite Naval Base.

The Japanese invasion forces swiftly swept the defenders of the Philippines before them. MacArthur fought a series of skillful delaying actions, retreating gradually into the narrow Bataan peninsula where there took place one of the most courageous defensive stands in American military history.

The men of Bataan had to stand alone against overwhelming odds. There was no hope of getting reinforcements or supplies to them, since the U.S. Pacific fleet lay shattered and the Royal Navy was licking its wounds and vainly trying to defend Singapore. The men on Bataan were almost without food. There were no replacements for damaged military equipment and few medical supplies, yet the Americans and Filipinos fought on. Half-starved and dying from disease and wounds, they were still able to make up a bitterly humorous verse about themselves and their hopeless situation. It went:

"We're the battered battlers of Bataan,
No mothers, no fathers, and no Uncle Sam!"

They had just one P-40 fighter plane to fly defensive missions for them. The battered battlers of Bataan called

This captured Japanese photograph shows victorious enemy troops on Bataan. (U.S. Army Photo)

this plane their "Air Force" and sent a wry message to the United States about it.

"Please send us another P-40," the message read. "Ours is full of holes."

In February President Roosevelt ordered General MacArthur to leave the Philippines. Churchill had done a similar thing when he had personally ordered Field Marshal Gort to leave Dunkirk. Neither general wanted to leave his men, but it was felt that the future services of MacArthur and Gort would be too valuable to let them be taken prisoner so early in the war.

MacArthur, his wife, and son were taken from Luzon in a motor torpedo boat under the command of Navy Lieutenant John Bulkeley. With them on the perilous journey through enemy waters was another general with whom little Arthur MacArthur played as the boat made its way to Mindanao. This was "General Tojo," the cook's monkey. The MacArthur party left Luzon on March 11 and arrived at Mindanao on March 13. From there the general was flown to Australia in a B-17. Upon his arrival in Australia General MacArthur pointed out that the President had ordered him to leave the Philippines. Then he added, "I came through, and I shall return!"

The men on Bataan held out until April 9. On that day more than 35,000 of the defending forces surrendered, but General Jonathan Wainwright and some of his men escaped to the nearby fortress on Corregidor.

The ordeal was not yet over for the men of Bataan who had surrendered. They were herded by their captors on a 200-mile death march to Camp O'Donnell in central Luzon. Almost a thousand thirst-crazed, starving Americans died on this march. The savage Japanese guards bayoneted anyone who fell from exhaustion. Hundreds more later died in prison.

General Jonathan M. Wainwright. (U.S. Army Photo)

Wainwright and his few remaining men held out on Corregidor until May 6. As he prepared to surrender his men Wainwright wrote, "We are being subjected to terrific air and artillery bombardment, and it is unreasonable to expect that we can hold out for long. We have done our best, both here and on Bataan, and although we are beaten we are still unashamed." In September 1945 Wainwright was awarded the Congressional Medal of Honor.

The survivors of Corregidor were thrown into Bilibad Prison in Manila where they, like the survivors of Bataan, died by the hundreds. In this prison there was one carefully guarded trophy. When the American flag was lowered in surrender at Corregidor it was burned to keep it from falling into the hands of the Japanese. Before he destroyed the colors, however, Colonel Paul Bunker cut a piece from the flag and sewed it under his shirt. He died in prison, but not before he had passed his treasured keepsake on to Colonel Delbert Ausmus. Ausmus also sewed the strip of flag under his shirt. After the war he turned it over to United States Secretary of War Robert Patterson, as Colonel Bunker had asked him to do. Today this piece of flag from the famous last stand at Corregidor in the Philippines is one of the most treasured mementos in the Army Museum at West Point.

For six seemingly endless months after Pearl Harbor, the Japanese scored victory after victory against the Allies. They captured Hong Kong on Christmas Day, 1941, after a two-week siege. On February 15, 1942, Singapore fell. This was a particularly hard blow, because Singapore had been thought impregnable. It had long been known as "the Gibraltar of the Pacific." The Japanese did not try to assault it from the sea. Instead, crack jungle troops filtered down through Malaya and captured the island fortress from the rear. Within a month the conquest of the

During the Japanese siege of Corregidor many of the gallant defenders lived in underground tunnels in "The Rock." The last submarine to contact Corregidor in May, 1942 picked up this picture. (U.S. Army Photo)

Dutch East Indies was completed. Parts of New Britain, New Guinea, and the Solomon Islands were captured, and Australia was in danger.

Burma was next on the Japanese schedule of conquest. Early in March the Japanese took the vital port of Rangoon, which British writer Rudyard Kipling had made famous in his poem "Mandalay." By May they had overrun most of Burma, capturing Lashio and cutting the Burma Road. This 800-mile road was a key Lend-Lease supply route to China.

During the fighting in Burma, American General Joseph W. Stilwell was named Chiang Kai-shek's chief of staff. "Vinegar Joe" Stilwell took command of two Chinese armies in Burma and tried to stem the tide of onrushing Japanese. Stilwell's forces were trapped in southern Burma, however, and had to retreat to Imphal, India. This forced march was made through roadless jungle, across flooded rivers, up and down steep mountains. It was hailed as an epic of courage in the face of great odds, but "Vinegar Joe" left no doubt in anybody's mind that it was a retreat, not a victory. Like MacArthur he promised to return — both men kept their words — but "Vinegar Joe" put it more bluntly.

"I claim we took a beating," he said. "We got run out of Burma. I think we ought to find out what caused it, and then go back and retake it."

The best record of an Allied combat unit in the early part of the Burma campaign was that of the "Flying Tigers" under Claire Chennault. Chennault, a leather-faced flying veteran, had been retired as a captain from the United States Army Air Forces in 1937 because of deafness. He was then 47. That same year Madame Chiang Kai-shek had persuaded him to help train the Chinese Air Force.

Chennault had a number of new ideas about aerial com-

A Flying Tiger fighter plane hidden by bamboo trees. (U.S. Air Force Photo)

bat tactics. He did not believe in fighter pilots fighting as individuals in lone "dog fights," as had often been the case in World War I. Instead, he believed in teamwork with two planes working together as a single unit. He now put these ideas into practice against the Japanese. Not only did he train Chinese pilots, but he flew with them into combat and unofficially shot down some 30 of the enemy.

Early in 1941, Chennault knew that the United States would soon be in the war. He persuaded the U.S. Department of State to let him recruit an American Volunteer Group of flyers to protect the Burma Road. One hundred and fifty of these volunteers from the U.S. Army Air Forces, the Marine Corps, and the Navy arrived in Burma in the fall of 1941. Their planes were 100 old P-40 fighters on the noses of which they painted tiger sharks' teeth. Only about half of these planes were ever ready for combat at any one time. In addition to their salaries, which ranged from $600 to $750 a month, the pilots were paid $500 by the Chinese government for every Japanese plane they shot down.

The Flying Tigers ran up a truly remarkable score of "kills" against the Japanese. Officially, bonuses were paid on 299 Japanese planes destroyed between December 1941 and July 1942 in the battle for Burma and the defense of the Burma Road. Unofficially some 1500 Japanese airmen were shot down during this period, against a loss of less than a dozen Flying Tiger pilots in combat. Eventually the American Volunteer Group was inducted into the U.S. Army Air Forces and Chennault was given a general's stars, but not before the name of the Flying Tigers had been written into legend in the skies over Burma.

When the Burma Road was finally cut by the Japanese, no Lend-Lease supplies could reach China by land. And, until the United States Navy could fight its way back across

The Hump over which supplies were flown to China. (U.S. Air Force Photo)

the Pacific, supplies could not be delivered by sea. If China were to be kept in the war, some way would have to be found to ferry in supplies by air.

It was decided to use U.S. Army Air Force C-47's flying over the "Hump" from India to China, crossing the high Himalayas at altitudes up to 20,000 feet. At first this seemed like an impossible feat. The trip would take five or six hours. The transport planes did not have pressurized cabins, so the crews would have to use oxygen much of the way. And the slow-flying transports would be able to do little to defend themselves against Japanese fighter attacks.

But a number of airmen were willing to risk their lives in the effort. In April 1942 ten C-47's ferried into China over the "Hump" a first historic cargo — 30,000 gallons of precious aviation gasoline. With the use of larger planes such as the four-engine C-54, the airlift tonnage gradually increased until it reached a total of 71,000 tons a month by the end of the war — far more than had been delivered monthly over the prewar Burma Road. This effort was not without cost in men and equipment. During the course of the war, 850 airmen were killed and 250 planes were destroyed flying over the "Hump."

The men who flew the first C-47's from India to China were not told why they were carrying only aviation gasoline. Most of them thought, of course, that it was for the remnants of the Chinese Air Force. This was not true. The gasoline was to be stored in China for possible use by Jimmy Doolittle's raiders — a daring group of flyers who were at that moment planning a secret mission to fly B-25's off a U.S. Navy carrier, bomb Tokyo, and then, if their luck held, fly on to China. There, if their luck still held and they were able to land their planes on temporary airfields, they would refuel and fly to Chungking.

Five

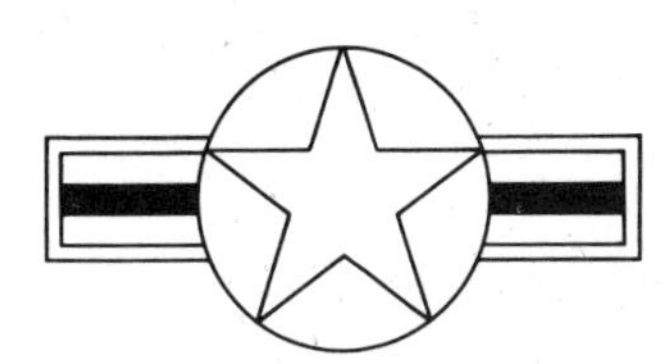

The Doolittle Raid on Tokyo

"Hap, do you think one of your medium bombers could take off in 500 feet?" Fleet Admiral Ernest King asked.

Hap Arnold thought a moment. "Maybe. If it was stripped down."

"How about with a bomb load?"

Again the commanding general of the Army Air Forces puzzled over the question. Finally he said, "Yes, I think so Why?"

Admiral King explained that one of his aides, Captain Francis Low, had recently suggested a carrier air strike against Japan. Carrier planes, however, only had a range of several hundred miles.

"He thinks long-range Army bombers might do the job," Admiral King said. "What do you think of the idea?"

Henry "Hap" Arnold had learned to fly back in Orville

General Henry H. Arnold. (U.S. Air Force Photo)

and Wilbur Wright's day. He was one of the first two Army men to do so. He had never turned down an idea simply because it was too daring. He did not do so now.

"I like it," he said simply.

As soon as Admiral King left the office, Hap Arnold began thinking about what man he should pick to plan such an attack. The man would have to have a great deal of technical know-how to modify whatever planes were used for the raid on Tokyo. He would also have to have special qualities of leadership and courage. The man who seemed to fit the bill was Lieutenant Colonel James Doolittle.

* * *

Jimmy Doolittle was one of the best-known stunt and racing flyers in the world. What many people did not know was that he was also an aeronautical engineer. No longer a young man, he had been developing his own special brand of courage and leadership all of his life.

James Harold Doolittle was born at Alameda, California, in 1896. While he was still a youngster he and his mother, Rosa, went with his father, Frank, to Nome, Alaska. The boy's father had dreams of discovering gold and becoming rich. These dreams never came true, and after a few years Jimmy's mother decided to take the boy back to California to school.

In grade school and high school in Los Angeles Jimmy became interested in three things — flying, boxing, and a girl named Josephine Daniels. After trying several times to build his own glider, Jimmy concentrated on boxing and trying to win Jo's affections. He was a successful boxer, but with Jo he seemed to be no more successful than he had been in building gliders. A small boy — fullgrown he was only five feet five inches tall — Jimmy nevertheless had great determination to succeed. He also had an almost perfect sense of balance. He won numerous high school boxing championships as well as college championships when he later attended the University of California. He fought professionally a number of times, until Jo told him she would never marry a boxer.

When the United States entered World War I in 1917, Jimmy's early desire to become a flyer returned. He also thought that Jo might find him more appealing in a flyer's uniform. He was right. He joined the aviation section of the Army Signal Corps, and he and Jo were married in Los Angeles in December 1917. On March 11, 1918, he was commissioned a second lieutenant.

Lieutenant Doolittle never got overseas in World War I. Despite his loud protests, he was sent to Louisiana for advanced flight training. Later he became a flight instructor at San Diego — the best flight instructor, said several of his superior officers, that the Air Service had.

After the war a number of Army flyers began a fight to create a separate air force. The leader in this fight was General William "Billy" Mitchell, who had been Chief of the Air Service under General John J. Pershing's First Army in France in 1918. Mitchell believed that the bomber had made seapower generally and the battleship in particular obsolete. To prove his point, Mitchell persuaded the United States Navy to let him test his theories in 1921.

Several captured German warships were anchored off Chesapeake Bay and bombers from Langley Field attacked and quickly sank them. Jimmy Doolittle was one of the pilots who trained at Langley Field for this test. The Navy refused to admit that this demonstration proved Mitchell's point. Later, in 1923, Air Service bombers also sank two obsolete U.S. battleships off Cape Hatteras, but Mitchell's futile feud with the Navy and Army continued.

In 1925 Mitchell was sent to San Antonio, Texas, as a

lieutenant colonel. There he continued to speak out against Army and Navy authorities. Finally he was court-martialled for giving a statement to the press that was sharply critical of the high command in Washington. He was found guilty and suspended from duty for five years. In 1926 Mitchell resigned from the Service. At his death in 1936 the United States still had no separate air arm.

Mitchell's fight was not in vain. Beginning in the late 1920's the development of aircraft carriers indicated the gradual acceptance of some of his theories about air power. Although the destruction of American battleships at Pearl Harbor seemed to be final proof of part of Mitchell's predictions, his belief that the bomber meant the end of all seapower was disproved when war came.

Jimmy Doolittle, like Mitchell, firmly believed that without air support from a separate air arm no modern army or navy could win a battle. But he went about getting air service recognition in a more constructive way. During the 1920's and 1930's he piloted planes in a number of spectacular air shows and air races to help make the nation aware of the airplane. He won the Mackay and Harmon trophies as well as the Schneider, Bendix, and Thompson trophy races. He also enrolled at the Massachusetts Institute of Technology, where he received his doctorate in aeronautical engineering.

It was Doolittle's advanced schooling that helped him make a little-known but vital contribution toward winning World War II when it finally came. Beginning in 1930, Doolittle went to work for the Shell Oil Company, keeping his reserve commission in the Army Air Force. In this civilian job Doolittle urged the Shell Oil Company to produce large quantities of high-octane fuel (gasoline with tetraethyl lead added to it) at its plant in Wood River, Illinois. He also urged the War Department to accept high-octane gasoline as its standard fuel. This fuel made possible greatly increased airplane engine power and speeds at high altitudes. The War Department finally adopted 100-octane gasoline as its standard fuel in 1938, certainly a vital element in deciding the air war over Europe and the Pacific.

With the United States on the brink of war, Jimmy Doolittle returned to active duty as a major in 1940 and was quickly promoted to lieutenant colonel.

On a sunny day in February 1942 Lieutenant Colonel Jimmy Doolittle stood before some 140 airmen at Eglin Field, Florida. All of these men had volunteered for an unknown secret mission. Doolittle did not tell them now what that secret mission was to be. He did tell them that it would be a dangerous one. He also gave them a chance to back out. None did.

"The first thing you're going to do," Doolittle said, "is to learn how to take off in a B-25 within 500 feet. And in case any of you have any doubts that it can be done, I'll tell you right now that I've already done it myself."

Doolittle had decided as soon as Hap Arnold had told him about the mission that the Army's medium bomber, the two-engine B-25, was the ship for the job. He had immediately gone to work with the engineers at Wright Field to remodel a practice ship. They had made the plane lighter in every possible way, replacing the heavy and costly Norden bombsight with a smaller, lighter, and cheaper device, and removing turrets and other equipment. This was the plane Doolittle had managed to get airborne in 500 feet, despite the fact that it was carrying cargo equal to the weight of extra gasoline and a full bomb load.

Five-hundred-feet markers were painted on the Eglin Field runways. A Navy carrier officer told the Army pilots how to take off quickly by keeping the landing flaps of their planes down and starting their runs with their engines at full throttle. The men practiced from dawn to dark. Gradually they learned to take off in the required distance.

Meanwhile their B-25's were being stripped of all dead weight. Extra gasoline tanks were installed. By March the crews and planes were ready for the secret mission. Still none of the men knew what that mission was to be, although they did know they would be dropping their bombs at a risky altitude of only 1,500 feet.

When Doolittle received word from the West Coast that all was in readiness there, he ordered his air crews to fly their B-25's to California. On April 1, 1942, a Navy carrier task force led by Admiral William "Bull" Halsey's *Enterprise* sailed from San Francisco. Sixteen awkward-looking B-25's were lashed to the decks of Captain Marc "Pete" Mitscher's aircraft carrier *Hornet*. Below decks eighty B-25 crew members were still puzzling over their destination. Doolittle did not make them wait any longer. As soon as the carrier was safely at sea he announced their destination — "Tokyo."

With more than two weeks at sea ahead of them, the air crews had plenty of time to worry about the dangers that lay ahead. Actually, however, as soon as they knew the purpose of all their intensive training, most of their fears left them. They had plenty of work to do, making sure their planes were in first-class condition, and being briefed on their exact targets. They knew, of course, that fuel was going to be one of their main worries. If the carrier could get them in as close as 400 miles from Tokyo, they could bomb the Japanese capital and make it to the Chinese airfields with gasoline to spare. If they had to take off any farther out than that, their fuel supply might not carry them to China.

Jimmy Doolittle's B-25 bombers aboard the U.S.S. Hornet on the way to Tokyo. (Navy Department Photo in the National Archives)

Early on the stormy morning of April 18 the worst happened. Cruisers accompanying the task force spotted a small Japanese ship. Although the enemy ship was quickly sunk by the *Northampton,* Halsey and Mitscher feared a radio message might have been sent alerting Tokyo. If so, the entire task force would be in danger. The Doolittle raiders would have to take off now — some 800 miles short of their intended take-off point.

Doolittle did not hesitate, nor did any of the B-25 crews. As an additional hazard, they would have to take off from a pitching carrier deck. Doolittle gave his crews a few last-minute instructions. Then, as a Navy man dropped the checkered flag waving him off, Doolittle led the way to Tokyo.

Doolittle made the take-off easily, and all fifteen of the other bombers followed his example. One or two almost crashed into the sea, but in a short time all were airborne and headed for their target, flying along on the "deck" at wavetop height to avoid radar detection.

Doolittle's plane hit the Japanese coast right on target and on schedule. Nearby his crew spotted other B-25's also on schedule. Several were attacked by Japanese fighter planes and shelled by anti-aircraft guns. The Doolittle raiders flew on relentlessly just above the housetops.

Suddenly Tokyo loomed before them. The planes now climbed to 1,500 feet. A moment later targets were spotted, bomb bays were opened, and the B-25's made the bombing run. As the bombs were released, the planes bucked like wild horses at the sudden lightening of their loads.

Now the problem was getting safely out of Japan. Until the very last minute before the raid, the United States State Department had been trying to get permission from Russia for the Doolittle raiders to land in Vladivostok aft-

Admiral William F. Halsey. (U.S. Army Photo)

er they bombed Tokyo. The B-25's used on the raid had even been offered as a Lend-Lease gift to the Soviet Union, but the request had been refused. Now the flyers had to try and find safe landing fields somewhere in China. Their planes were short of fuel and night was coming on.

In the lead plane Jimmy Doolittle flew on until he knew they had crossed the East China Sea and were over the China coast. Then, with darkness closing in, bad weather obscuring the land below, and his ship running out of fuel, he climbed to 10,000 feet and ordered his crew to bail out.

Doolittle and all of his crew landed safely. They managed to walk to Chu Chow, the airfield where they had intended to land. From Chu Chow they were taken by Chinese troops to Chunking where Madame Chiang Kai-shek greeted them. There they began to learn what had happened to the rest of the Doolittle raiders.

All of the planes had completed the raid. Several planes landed in Japanese territory and the crews were taken prisoner. Some of these men, it was later learned, were executed. Others died in prison. Most of the other planes landed in China, but many of these men were wounded from attacks by Japanese Zeros during the raid or injured when their planes crash-landed. Several men were killed in crash landings. Those who survived were taken to Chunking by Chinese guerrilla forces.

It would be months, and even years in some instances, before the gallant band of Doolittle's raiders would make its way back to the United States. And nine of the eighty men who made the raid would never return home.

The attack had taken Japan completely by surprise. Serious fires were started and there was panic in Tokyo. Many persons were killed, including a number of Japanese marines who had been training in the city.

While the damage caused by the raid was slight compared with later bombings, its morale-boosting value in the United States and its morale-damaging effects in Japan were great. The Japanese had been hearing about nothing except Japanese victories and now their homeland had been bombed. What might happen next?

Americans realized that the attack would scarcely decide the war. Nevertheless, they were heartened by the valor and daring of the men who made it. They squared their shoulders and went back to work with more determination and zeal than ever before to provide the men and material for a *real* blow at the Japanese. And the next one wouldn't come from "Shangri-La," the fictional spot from which President Roosevelt had said Doolittle's raiders had launched their mission.

Lieutenant Colonel Doolittle was promoted to brigadier general and awarded the Congressional Medal of Honor for leading the raid. His epic exploits did not end then. In the months ahead he was to become the combat commander of first the Twelfth and finally the Eighth Air Force and play a leading role in defeating the *Luftwaffe* in Europe.

* * *

The Tokyo raid made the Japanese decide to attack and destroy the United States carriers that made attacks on the Japanese homeland possible. To do this, they split up their own naval task forces, sending two of their big carriers into the Coral Sea and their other four big carriers toward Midway Island. They also launched a diversionary attack on the Aleutian Islands, landing troops at Kiska and Attu where they were to remain until 1943, when United States soldiers finally drove them out.

All of these plans were known by the United States just as soon as they were made. The United States was still

General James H. Doolittle. (U.S. Air Force Photo)

breaking the Japanese code, and the Japanese plans were told to Admiral Chester W. Nimitz, who had taken over as Commander in Chief of the United States Pacific Fleet from Admiral Kimmel ten days after Pearl Harbor. Nimitz decided to meet the Japanese head on, both in the Coral Sea and off Midway.

In the Coral Sea area the Japanese planned to land invasion troops at Port Moresby in New Guinea, and at Tulagi, capital of the Solomons. They did not intend, at this time, to invade Australia, where General MacArthur had set up a plan of defense and the United States had sent a number of troops and military supplies. The Japanese intended only to isolate Australia, cutting it off from all further Allied aid.

The Battle of the Coral Sea was the first naval engagement in which opposing warships did not exchange a shot. All damage was done by aircraft flying from carriers. The main engagement took place on May 8 when planes from both task forces attacked each other's main carriers at the same time. Navy dive bombers damaged the Japanese carrier *Shokaku* so severely that the ship was put out of action. A second large Japanese carrier, the *Zuikaku,* lost most of its planes. At the same time both U.S. carriers were hit. The *Yorktown* was damaged, and uncontrollable fires were started aboard the *Lexington,* which had finally to be abandoned and was ordered sunk by the U.S. destroyer *Phelps.*

Although the actual score in this historic battle favored the Japanese, it was a strategic victory for the United States. Vital Port Moresby was saved, and, most important of all, the uninterrupted advance southeastward by the Japanese was finally brought to a halt.

Admiral Yamamoto, the man who had planned the Pearl Harbor raid, personally led the assault on Midway Island which began on June 3. Land-based United States Army,

The U.S. Lexington burning, following the Battle of the Coral Sea. (Navy Department Photo in the National Archives)

Fire and damage aboard the U.S.S Yorktown during the Battle of Midway. (Navy Department Photo in the National Archives)

Navy, and Marine Corps planes located and attacked the Japanese ships when they were still 600 miles from Midway. The next day planes from the four Japanese carriers bombed Midway. Army and Marine flyers fought off the bombers while the American carriers launched their first air strikes against the Japanese carriers. These strikes were led by Lieutenant Commander John Waldron's heroic Torpedo Squadron Eight, whose members had become close friends of the Doolittle raiders when they had been aboard the *Hornet* just a few weeks earlier on their way to Tokyo. Only one of the thirty-six members of Torpedo Squadron Eight, Ensign George Gay, survived the Battle of Midway. Gay was severely wounded and shot down into the sea, but he survived by hiding under a rubber seat cushion from the strafing Zeros. Picked up after dark, Gay gave an eyewitness account of the day's battle, which he had seen while floating in the sea.

Navy dive bombers next attacked the Japanese, sinking the large carriers *Akagi, Kaga,* and *Soryu*. The Japanese struck back with bombs and torpedoes, damaging the U.S. carrier *Yorktown* so severely that the ship was abandoned. Later it was sunk by an enemy submarine. Late in the afternoon, U.S. aircraft from the *Enterprise* hit and sank the *Hiryu,* the fourth and last of the large Japanese carriers.

The Battle of Midway was over, and Pearl Harbor had been avenged; all four of the enemy carriers which had launched the attack on Pearl Harbor just six months earlier were sunk at Midway. In addition to the carriers, Japanese losses were one cruiser and 258 aircraft. U.S. losses were one carrier, one destroyer, and 132 aircraft. The Japanese had suffered their first decisive defeat in one of the most important naval battles in history. The Battle of Midway was the turning point of the war in the Pacific.

Six

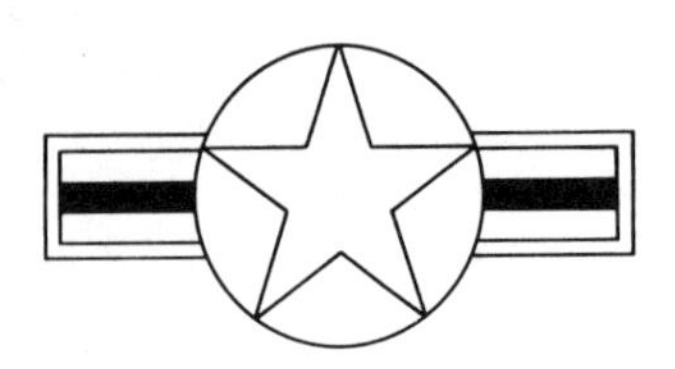

Eisenhower Takes Command

The newspapermen who spelled his name "Ersenbeing" after the Louisiana Army maneuvers in 1941 might not have known Dwight D. Eisenhower, but his fellow officers did. They knew and respected "Ike" as an outstanding military man. Shortly after the Louisiana maneuvers he was promoted to brigadier general, and a few days after the United States went to war Army Chief of Staff George C. Marshall called Ike to Washington.

Eisenhower was disappointed when he received Marshall's call. He wanted to remain with his troops in the field and not be tied to a desk. World War I had ended the day before he was to be sent overseas, and he definitely did not want to miss the boat this time.

Ike knew why he was being called to Washington. Between 1935 and 1939 he had been in the Philippines as senior assistant to General MacArthur. With the Philippines now under siege by the Japanese, General Marshall needed an aide who had first-hand knowledge of the area.

In Washington Eisenhower was asked to take charge of getting whatever help was possible to the beleaguered battlers of Bataan. Despite his great sympathy for the people of the Philippines, as well as his close kinship with the army defenders, Eisenhower knew almost immediately that the best that could be done there was to fight a delaying action. The lifeline to Australia must be kept open, however, so that country could eventually be used as a base from which to counterattack the Japanese.

Ike and his staff bent all of their efforts, in the next weeks, toward getting a trickle of supplies into Bataan with the use of submarines, and toward getting major military reinforcements to Australia. The success in getting troops to Australia was partly due to the use of such British ships as the *Queen Mary* as troop transports. The *Queen Mary* could carry 14,000 men and was fast enough to travel unescorted through enemy waters.

General Marshall also asked Eisenhower during this period for his ideas about how the global war should be fought. Ike told the Chief of Staff that he thought the United States should first work as a partner with England to defeat the Axis powers in Europe and then concentrate on defeating Japan. Ike pointed out that if the United States tried first to defeat Japan, ignoring the war in Europe, England might fall. England, Ike felt, should be used as the platform from which to launch an attack against Nazi-held Europe.

Marshall agreed with these ideas and so did President Roosevelt, Prime Minister Churchill, and the other American and British military leaders who met in Washington during December 1941 and January 1942 at what was

General Dwight D. Eisenhower. (U.S. Army Photo)

known as the Arcadia conference. At this meeting a Combined Chiefs of Staff was set up to direct the Anglo-American war effort. This committee consisted of the top Army, Navy, and Air Force leaders of Great Britain and the United States.

To fit in with the Combined Chiefs, the United States organized a committee called the Joint Chiefs of Staff. This group included the Chief of Staff of the Army, General Marshall; Commander of the Army Air Forces, General Henry H. Arnold; Chief of Naval Operations, Admiral Ernest J. King; and the President's personal aide, Admiral William D. Leahy, who acted as chairman.

The Combined Chiefs held frequent meetings in Washington and elsewhere throughout the war. In addition, China's Chiang Kai-shek and Russia's Joseph Stalin also met with Roosevelt, Churchill, and the other members of the Combined Chiefs at the important Teheran and Yalta conferences.

It was one thing, of course, to work out plans on how the war should be fought and quite another thing to provide the men and material to fight such a war. In describing the situation as far as the Air Forces were concerned, Hap Arnold said, "We've got plenty of plans but no planes." Much the same thing could have been said about the rest of the American war effort at this time. During the next few months, however, the armed services and civilian workers began to perform twin miracles of training men and producing military supplies.

Although many men volunteered, the armed services depended mainly on the draft for their manpower. Men between the ages of 18 and 45 were now included in the draft, and they were required to serve until six months after the war had ended.

On Pearl Harbor Sunday there were just over a million

and a half officers and men in the Army. This number was to grow to more than eight million men by the end of the war. The Navy grew from less than half a million to almost three and a half million, the Marines from about 65,000 to about half a million, and the Coast Guard from 25,000 to 170,000.

At the start of the war there were some 200,000 officers and men in the Army Air Forces. This number grew to almost two and a half million by war's end. The number of operational planes increased from 2,500 to 80,000. Navy and Marine flying personnel increased from about 50,000 to half a million.

Total war became a reality to the American people when, for the first time in the nation's history, women were accepted by the Armed Forces. The Women's Army Auxiliary Corps (WAAC) was created on May 14, 1942. It became a regular part of the Army on July 1, 1943, and was renamed the Women's Army Corps (WAC). Some 17,000 members of the WAC served overseas. Navy WAVE's, Coast Guard SPAR's, Air Force WAF's, and members of the Marine women's auxiliary also saw important duty at home and overseas. In all more than 200,000 American women served in the Armed Forces, and many of them were decorated.

The next job was to mobilize American industry. Billions of dollars had been appropriated for rearmament but little had been done to mass-produce guns, tanks, planes, munitions, and the countless other essential tools of war. What little had been produced had been given to other Allied nations through Lend-Lease. President Roosevelt now called upon American industry and the American people to produce as they never had before. The response was electric and the results spectacular.

The output of steel and aluminum increased tremend-

WACS landing in North Africa. (U.S. Army Photo)

A nurse digging a slit trench near Anzio, Italy. (U.S. Army Photo)

ously. A synthetic rubber industry was created almost overnight, to make up for the loss of natural rubber from Japanese-held Malaya and Indonesia. New war plants were built by the hundreds. By 1943 more than half of the nation's industry had been converted to war production. Planes, tanks, and trucks were manufactured by the automobile industry. Radar sets were produced by radio manufacturers. Vacuum cleaner plants made machine guns. New shipbuilding methods were used to produce "Liberty" ships by the score.

Total war was brought home to the American people as more than two million of the nation's women went to work in war plants. "Rosie the Riveter" played a key role in producing everything from an odd-looking little "midget reconnaissance car," that was to gain world fame as the Jeep, to the giant workhorse of a bomber, the B-24, both of which began coming from the assembly lines early in the war.

By 1942 American war production equalled that of the Axis powers. By the end of the war it was more than twice as great. For the Normandy invasion alone some 750,000 tons of supplies a month were shipped to England through 1943. This figure grew to almost two million tons a month by D-Day, June 6, 1944.

In order to perform this miracle of production it was necesssary for the government to set up a number of wartime controls. These included the rationing of scarce foods and goods; price, salary, and rent controls; and the censorship of mail between the United States and other countries. Some of the government agencies that were established to handle these controls and to mobilize the nation's resources included the Office of Price Administration (OPA), the War Production Board (WPB), the Office of Economic Stabilization (OES), and the Office of War Mobilization (OWM).

Civilian men and women also did volunteer work to aid the war effort. They acted as air raid wardens, knitted and sewed and supervised blood donations for the Red Cross, served without pay on draft and rationing boards, and took part in the activities of the United Service Organization (USO) that helped entertain service men. Housewives raised their own vegetables in Victory Gardens, and dutifully saved their tin cans, waste paper, and fats. The United States was fighting the greatest war in its history, and the American people responded as they had always done to such a challenge. After the war, officials generally agreed that American production had made victory possible.

In May 1942 General Marshall sent General Eisenhower on an inspection trip to England to decide how that nation could be used as a military base to train men and to stage the invasion of the continent. Upon his return to the United States in June, Eisenhower told Marshall that for some time to come the American offensive from England would have to consist of air raids. He put his other observations into a written report for Marshall to give to the officer who would be in charge of American operations in England.

"Who do you think that man should be?" Marshall asked.

"General McNarney," Eisenhower replied.

"It may be you," Marshall said. "If so, how soon can you leave?"

A few days later General Dwight Eisenhower was named American commander of the European theater of war. Within less than two years he would lead the Allied forces in their assault on Normandy in the greatest amphibious invasion in history.

* * *

Dwight David Eisenhower had come a long way in the military career his mother and father had not wanted him to follow. Like all wise parents, however, the senior Eisenhowers had let their son choose his own career. Eventually it would lead to the White House.

Dwight Eisenhower was born at Denison, Texas, on October 14, 1890, but he grew up in Abilene, Kansas. He was one of six brothers — a seventh died in infancy — in a family that believed firmly in strong religious training and hard work. His mother, Ida, and his father, David, were members of a church group called the Brethren in Christ that was somewhat similar to the Quakers.

"Little Ike," as he was always called by his boyhood friends, attended the grade and high schools in Abilene. In many ways he was a typical Midwest American boy. He played basketball and football on the school teams and was a better than average student. His favorite subject was history, and he particularly liked to read about military campaigns.

In addition to his school activities, Ike mowed lawns, delivered newspapers, and worked in a creamery to earn spending money. One year he left high school to work full-time to help his brother Edgar, who was called "Big Ike," get through college. There was always a strong family loyalty among the brothers, a loyalty that was to last all of their lives.

"Little Ike," who by now was taller than "Big Ike," graduated from high school in 1909. He worked for a year and then took the examinations to enter West Point. He had wanted to go to Annapolis, but he was too old. In 1911 he was admitted to West Point.

At the military academy he became a star football halfback until he injured his knee and was forced to give up the game. Still not much better than an average student, Ike stood 61st in a class of 164 when he was graduated and commissioned a second lieutenant on June 12, 1915.

Lieutenant Eisenhower now began many Army years as an apprentice to become thoroughly trained in the soldier's craft. Just as there had been nothing spectacular in his work as a student, there was nothing spectacular in his early work as an Army officer. But he did advance steadily and surely, learning as he went. And he had one very special quality, his remarkable ability to get along with people, to like and respect them and to be liked and respected in return.

While stationed at Fort Sam Houston in San Antonio, Texas, Eisenhower met Mamie Geneva Doud. On July 1, 1916, Ike was promoted to first lieutenant and on that same day he and Mamie were married. They had two sons — Doud, who died in infancy, and John, who was to follow an Army career like his father.

During World War I Ike was promoted to the permanent grade of captain and worked to develop the new Army Tank Corps. After the war he was made a major, a field officer grade in which he remained for the next sixteen years. During these hard, lean years in which the American people ignored their Armed Forces, Ike held firm to his belief that one day the nation would again call upon the Army for help; when that time came, he would be ready.

He continued his work with the Tank Corps until he was assigned to an infantry command in the Panama Canal Zone. Next he was sent to the Army Command and General Staff School. Here he was no average student. He graduated first in his class. Later he attended the Army War College, did staff work in Washington, and was finally assigned as an assistant to General MacArthur, then Army Chief of Staff. The two men worked together in Washington trying to alert the nation to the need for mechanizing the nation's Armed Forces. When MacArthur was made military adviser to the Philippines, he took Eisenhower with him to Manila.

In the Philippines Ike continued to broaden his background for the important Army leadership that he knew would be needed in the future. He had become completely convinced of the vital role that the airplane would play in the next war. He organized a Filipino Air Force, learning to fly himself at the age of 47. Finally he was promoted to the rank of lieutenant colonel.

When World War II began in Europe, both Eisenhower and MacArthur agreed that sooner or later the United States would become involved. Ike thought, however, that the Japanese would not strike until the United States began to fight Hitler's Nazis and Mussolini's Fascists. In December 1939 Eisenhower was recalled to the United States. When he and MacArthur said goodbye in Manila they did not realize that, before they met again, MacArthur would have to fight and win a war in the Pacific and Eisenhower would have to fight and win a war in Europe.

Eisenhower and his assistant, General Mark Clark, and their staff arrived in London in late June 1942. They went immediately to work organizing "Operation Bolero," the buildup and training of troops to invade the continent. This invasion, originally called "Operation Roundup," was tentatively scheduled for late 1942 or early 1943. Ike was certain, however, that the invasion would not be possible until 1944.

Seven

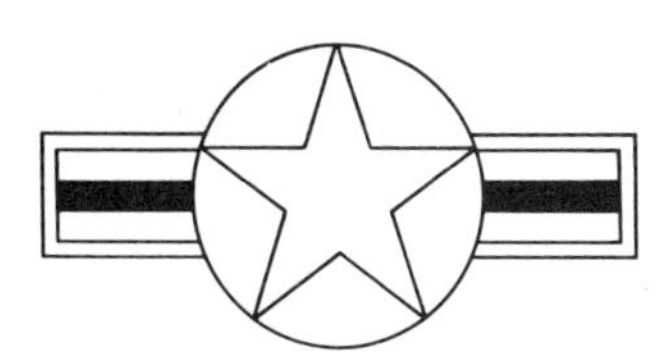

Operation Torch

"Whatever these Yank chaps want, give it to them! If we don't have it, get it! If we can't get it, make it!"

This was the order given to the members of one Royal Air Force base in England shortly before the arrival of the first American air crews in the United Kingdom. The spirit behind the order was typical of the attitude of friendly cooperation that usually existed between the American and English forces.

There were exceptions and misunderstandings, to be sure. Sometimes British troops complained that there were three things wrong with the Yanks: "They're overfed, they're overpaid, and they're over here." American G.I.'s promptly replied by threatening to cut loose the countless barrage balloons that were tethered over England "and let your island sink." For the most part, however, the Anglo-American partnership was remarkably successful at both low and high levels.

When they first got to England, many American troops were taken on tours through badly bombed sections of cities to see how the British had fared during the *blitz*. Many G.I.'s were invited into British homes for weekends. On such trips they were instructed by their unit commanders to take food with them, since most British families could easily use up a whole month's ration coupons feeding one hungry Yank.

Generous by nature, the G.I.'s needed little urging before they began giving away their own rations of candy and chewing gum to the English children, many of whom had not seen such sweets since the war began. And some youngsters had never seen them. Soon English children were greeting the Yanks everywhere with the query, "Got any gum, chum?"

Gradually American soldiers began to form fast friendships with their British comrades-in-arms, even to the point of adopting much of their slang. American flyers began to speak of a hard-fought mission as "a wizard party" in which some of their unfortunate wounded or shot down fellow flyers had "bought it" or "got the hammer."

Anglo-American cooperation started almost immediately in the air war as members of the Eighth Air Force had the chance to strike the first American blow against western Europe. The Eighth Air Force was led by General Carl "Tooey" Spaatz with General Ira Eaker in charge of the Eighth's bomber command. The Fifteenth Bombardment Squadron trained with the R.A.F. in A-20's (called "Bostons" by the British). To celebrate July 4, 1942, six crews from the Fifteenth led by Captain Charles Kegelman and accompanied by the R.A.F. bombed airfields in Holland. General Eisenhower visited with these crews be-

A Douglas A-20 is caught by flak and swerves out of control.

Seconds later the attack bomber dives to its doom in smoke and spray. (U.S. Air Force Photos)

fore and after their mission. Two American planes were shot down.

The first American heavy bomber raid was flown by the Ninety-seventh Bombardment Group on August 17, 1942. General Eaker led this twelve plane raid in a B-17 called the *Yankee Doodle*. All of the Flying Fortresses returned after successfully bombing railroad yards at Rouen, France. There were 160 Americans in this raid. By the end of the war, as many as 25,000 men would take part in a single heavy bomber mission against Germany.

During the rest of August and September the Eighth Air Force flew a number of other successful, if short-range missions, losing just two planes. The low loss rate was due in part to the tremendous fire power of the Fortresses, which carried ten fifty-caliber machine guns. It was mainly due, however, to the close fighter support given the raids by R.A.F. Spitfires.

The daylight bombing raids were temporarily halted by bad weather and by the sudden need to transfer many of the Eighth's bombers to General Jimmy Doolittle's Twelfth Air Force. The Twelfth was to give air support to a new invasion plan that had just been decided upon by the high command. This was "Operation Torch," the invasion of North Africa.

Torch was the first major amphibious operation in the European theater of war. It was decided upon for a number of reasons. The main reason was that an immediate large-scale invasion of the continent was impossible, despite demands for it by the Russians who were still fighting a desperate defensive battle on the eastern front.

When Eisenhower had first arrived in England there were only one American infantry division, one armored division, and advance units of the Air Force training in the United Kingdom. Since his arrival the Bolero buildup

An Eighth Air Force aerial gunner in action. (U.S. Air Force Photo)

had increased the number of available troops, but there was still a great lack of men and equipment. The shortage of landing barges was particularly severe.

One of the reasons for these shortages was the success that German submarines were having in attacking Allied shipping in the Atlantic. Before United States Chief of Naval Operations Ernest King and his British partners brought the German submarines under control in 1943, the Allies lost more than ten million tons of shipping. The American merchant marine alone lost more than 5,000 men during the course of the war. The submarine wolf packs were finally defeated by escorting convoys with destroyers and cruisers and by the use of carrier aircraft. Special airborne radar devices for locating the enemy undersea raiders were also effective.

At first Eisenhower was not in favor of invading North Africa. The Allies had set their sights on invading the continent, and he did not want them to set their sights elsewhere for fear the plan to assault the continent might be permanently postponed. He favored establishing a small bridgehead in France and then gradually enlarging it. After the war Eisenhower admitted that this move ("Operation Sledgehammer") would have been a mistake at the time.

Late in the summer of 1942 the Allies learned a bitter lesson about how costly an invasion of France might be. On August 19 a force of 6,000 men under joint British-Canadian command staged a miniature invasion of Dieppe on the Channel coast. The attack was a disaster in terms of the number of men lost, although many valuable lessons were learned for the invasion of Normandy which would be staged less than two years later.

Most of the Dieppe raiders were Canadian. Some 1,000 were British, and 50 were American Rangers. The most daring raid on the continent up to this time had been a British Commando assault on St. Nazaire in March 1942. The St. Nazaire raid had been made to blow up the Normandy docks in the harbor which took care of the *Tirpitz,* the only big battleship left in the German fleet since the *Bismarck* had been sunk. Though it was successful, the St. Nazaire effort had been merely a 600-man hit-and-run attack. The Dieppe raid was intended to capture a number of German landing barges if possible and to fully test the enemy defenses. The Allied forces were ashore for nine hours.

When the Dieppe raid was over almost 1,000 Canadians had been killed, and about 2,000 taken prisoner — more prisoners than the Canadians lost in the later Italian and European campaigns combined. The fact that it had taken more than 250 ships and sixty-seven squadrons of airplanes to make such a comparatively small-scale assault — and one that ended in failure at that — made Allied planners think twice about launching a full-scale invasion at this time.

Some sort of offensive move had to be made by the Allies, however, and British planners urged the assault on North Africa. If successful, such an attack would open the Mediterranean to Allied shipping and destroy the Axis forces threatening Egypt.

After the fall of France early in the war, the Axis had conquered Yugoslavia and Greece. The island of Crete in the Mediterranean had then been taken. England lost many men and much military equipment in Greece and on Crete. Far more serious, however, had been the threatened loss of the Mediterranean. Although the British still held Gibraltar and the island of Malta, it was suicidal for supply ships to run the entire length of the Mediterranean gantlet. This meant that the bulk of Allied supplies to support the British forces in the Middle East had to be sent all the way around the Cape of Good Hope at the southern tip of Africa.

In North Africa the British had been fighting a seesaw series of battles with the Italians and Germans since 1940. The final goal of the Axis was the Allied lifeline in this area, the Suez Canal, and the oil-rich lands of the Middle East. In the spring of 1942 the Italian and German armies had successfully entered Egypt, but the British Eighth Army made a heroic stand at El Alamein, just a few miles west of Alexandria. El Alamein proved to be the turning point in the war for the British.

At this point General Bernard L. Montgomery took command of the Eighth Army. On October 23, the day before some of the troops engaged in the Torch operation sailed for Africa, Montgomery counterattacked at El Alamein. Using 300 American Sherman tanks that had been landed at Port Said, Montgomery's "Desert Rats," as they liked to be called, began to drive German Field Marshal Erwin Rommel's *Afrika Korps* westward in defeat toward Libya. If Torch was successful, "Desert Fox" Rommel's forces would be trapped between the Torch invaders advancing eastward and Montgomery's forces advancing westward. Once the Axis was driven from the southern shores of the Mediterranean, the Allies would have a firm base for attacking southern Europe.

After the victory at El Alamein, the British attacked Tobruk. This small but vital Mediterranean seaport had first been captured by the Australians from the Italians early in the war. During the course of the war it changed hands five times.

In 1941 the "Aussies" had been ordered to hold the besieged seaport for two months. Against great odds the gallant defenders held it for eight months.

In June 1942, however, Rommel's forces had slashed

through the defenses and captured some 25,000 prisoners.

Tobruk was the hub around which the entire North African campaign would have to turn. British and Australian troops successfully recaptured it in November 1942, thus forging the first link in what it was hoped would be a chain of victories leading to final triumph in North Africa.

It was also hoped that the North African invasion would relieve some of the pressure on the Russians, who were locked in a desperate struggle with the Nazis at Stalingrad (now Volgograd). The Nazis had begun their attack on Stalingrad in late August of 1942. Incredible street fighting followed, as the Russians defended the city virtually brick by brick. A few days after Torch began, the Russians counterattacked north and south of Stalingrad. Hitler refused to let his army retreat from the center of the giant pincers movement that threatened to trap thousands of German troops. The result was victory for the Russians and disaster for the Germans.

Although the fighting in this area of Russia continued for many months, Stalingrad was eventually saved, and the Germans lost hundreds of thousands of troops that could never be replaced. Stalingrad was the Midway Island of the eastern front.

The invasion of French North Africa began on November 8, 1942. General Eisenhower was made commander-in-chief of the operation. It was hoped that the French military leaders and government officials in North Africa would greet the invaders as liberators if they were mainly American and led by an American general. For weeks U.S. State Department official Robert D. Murphy had been carrying on secret negotiations with the French in Africa to pave the way for a smooth Allied entry, and shortly before the invasion General Mark Clark had secretly contacted

French army officers to test their reactions to Torch. The French African forces, however, were loyal to Marshal Pétain and his government at Vichy in France, and no one could tell in advance whether or not they would resist the landings.

Landings were made near Casablanca in French Morocco and near Oran and Algiers in Algeria. The Casablanca forces included three armored divisions led by General George "Blood-and-Guts" Patton. These men had sailed directly from the United States. The Oran and Algiers forces, led by General Charles Ryder and General Lloyd Fredenhall, had sailed from England. American paratroops made their first combat jump at Oran. In all, about 100,000 troops, three-quarters of them American, took part in the landings. More than 800 ships were used, and about 1,000 planes flew air support missions from Gibraltar and off the decks of carriers. About 1,000 Allied troops were killed in the invasion, including 770 Americans and 240 British.

Patton's forces met strong resistance from tough French troops at Casablanca. Fighting in the area continued for several days, but finally on November 11 the French commander surrendered the city. Some resistance was met at Oran, but that city, too, surrendered on November 10. Almost no resistance was met at Algiers, and here the Allies had a stroke of good luck. Admiral Jean Darlan, commander of Vichy's armed forces, was in Algiers visiting his son who was ill. Darlan was captured by the Allies and turned over to General Eisenhower when Ike arrived from Gibraltar where he had been directing the invasion.

Ike, General Mark Clark, General Jimmy Doolittle and other members of the commander-in-chief's staff had been flown to the Gibraltar command post in six B-17's several days before the invasion. Jimmy Doolittle's luck had almost run out when the Fortress in which he was flying, piloted by Lieutenant John Summers, was attacked by several JU-88's and almost shot down into the sea. Eisenhower's plane, the *Red Gremlin,* was piloted by Major Paul Tibbets, who late in the war was to fly a truly historic bombing mission against Japan in a ship called the *Enola Gay*.

The Germans and Italians were taken completely by surprise by the invasion of North Africa, but they reacted quickly. Pétain's Vichy government denounced the Allied attack, and Hitler ordered his troops to occupy the whole of France. To prevent the French fleet at Toulon from being seized by the Germans, French naval officers sank their own ships. When Darlan in Africa was told that the Germans had occupied all of France, he immediately declared that Hitler had broken the armistice terms of 1940. He ordered all French resistance to the Allies in North Africa to cease. Eisenhower then named Darlan as the French political leader of North Africa, but the unfortunate Darlan did not have long to live. He was assassinated by a young French patriot on December 24.

Political problems continued to plague the Allies in North Africa. After Darlan's death, French General Henri Giraud was named Commissioner of North Africa to work with the American forces there. Giraud's leadership was not acknowledged, however, by French General Charles de Gaulle.

General de Gaulle had been in command of an armored division when Germany attacked France in 1940. When France fell and Pétain signed the truce with Hitler, de Gaulle refused to accept his government's actions. He fled to London where he announced defiantly, "France has lost a battle, but she has not lost the war!" The underground resistance movement in France used de Gaulle's words as a rallying cry.

Eisenhower had not included de Gaulle in the planning of Torch, however, because the military men of the French African forces disliked him. In fact they said he was disloyal, since he had not followed his government's orders as they had. Gradually, however, de Gaulle forced his will upon them. For a time he and Giraud were co-presidents of the French Committee of Liberation in Algiers. Later de Gaulle became the sole president and head of the French armed forces.

Following the successful landings in North Africa, the Allies rapidly built up their forces for the Battle of Tunisia which soon followed. Within a few weeks some 200,000 men, as well as hundreds of thousands of tons of supplies, had been landed in North Africa. General Eisenhower put a great deal of pressure on officials in Washington to send additional trucks to Africa. Some 5,400 of the vital vehicles finally arrived. With them was a message to Ike from his friend General Wilhelm D. Styer, who had arranged for the emergency shipment. It read, "If you should happen to want the Pentagon shipped over there, please try to give us about a week's notice."

Late in 1942 and early in 1943 the Axis partners also built up their forces in Tunisia, bringing in more than 150,000 troops. Rommel had been retreating westward through Libya before the determined advance of the British Eighth Army. Soon Rommel's *Afrika Korps* and the Axis reinforcements pouring into Tunisia joined at a series of defenses called the Mareth Line along the Tunisia-Libya border. Rommel now had Montgomery on one side of him and part of three American divisions at his rear. The crafty Desert Fox was not finished fighting, however. Far from it, in fact. He now turned suddenly on the Americans and soundly defeated them at Kasserine Pass. This was the first heavy fighting in which the American troops had engaged, and the green G.I.'s panicked in the face of Rommel's seasoned veterans. About 200 Americans were killed, but more than 2,000 were wounded and some 2,500 were taken prisoner.

There was much criticism of American troops after this incident, but General Eisenhower kept his faith in the G.I.'s. He knew they would prove themselves before the campaign was many weeks older. The G.I.'s repaid Ike's faith in them with a real feeling of devotion for him. A typical example of this feeling was shown one day when Ike had to fly to the front and told his orderly, Sergeant Michael McKeogh, that he needn't bother to come along. The weather was bad, and the trip promised to be a rough one.

"Mickey," Ike said, "I'm going to return tomorrow, and I won't need you before then. There's no use in both of us being uncomfortable."

Sergeant McKeogh looked squarely at Ike and said, "Sir, my mother wrote me that my job in this war was to take care of you. And she said also, 'If General Eisenhower doesn't come back from the war, don't *you* dare to come back.' "

Sergeant McKeogh accompanied Ike on the trip.

Another kind of faith was shown by four chaplains during this part of the North African campaign. Two of them were Protestants — George L. Fox and Clark V. Poling, whose father was the famous editor of the *Christian Herald*. The third was a Roman Catholic, John P. Washington, and the fourth was a Jew, Alexander D. Goode. The four men-of-good-will displayed their courage and faith in God when the Africa-bound troopship on which they were sailing was torpedoed off the coast of Greenland on February 3, 1943. They not only encouraged the panicky G.I.'s to jump from the stricken ship and be saved by approaching rescue craft, but they also passed out all

The dreaded German 88mm. gun in firing position in North Africa. Originally an anti-aircraft gun, it was first tested by the Germans in the Spanish Civil War in 1936. The 88 was the best all-around piece of Nazi artillery. (U.S. Army Photo)

the available life jackets. When all of the life jackets were gone, the chaplains gave away the ones they were wearing. When last seen, the four men of God had linked their arms together, and they were kneeling on the deck and praying as the ship sank beneath the waves.

The four chaplains were posthumously awarded Distinguished Service Crosses, and General William Arnold said of their selfless deed, "Their example has inspired and strengthened men everywhere. Men of all faiths can be proud that these men of different faiths died together."

Although chaplains were technically noncombatants during World War II, of the almost 9,000 men who served in this role more than 1,700 of them were awarded almost 2,500 decorations.

* * *

The American defeat at Kasserine Pass took place in February 1943. A few days later Rommel was driven back through the pass, and his career in Africa was about at an end. In March Montgomery's Eighth Army overwhelmed the Mareth Line, and Rommel's forces were pushed into a Bataan-like pocket in northeastern Tunisia. Rommel himself was relieved of his command and flown back to Germany.

The Axis forces now had their backs to the sea and were hammered relentlessly by the Allies. The main American offensive efforts were made by 100,000 troops led by General Omar Bradley. Men of the Thirty-fourth Division distinguished themselves by capturing such rugged defense positions as Hill 609 on the way to Mateur and Bizerte. Hill 609 was in the hands of crack German troops, but the Yanks stormed it and held their gains in the face of vicious German counterattacks. The G.I.'s of the Thirty-fourth Division thus regained much of the American honor and prestige that had been lost at Kasserine Pass.

By May the British captured Tunis, the Americans cap-

General Omar N. Bradley. (U.S. Army Photo)

tured Bizerte, and, with the surrender of the Axis in the Bon peninsula, all of North Africa was in Allied hands. The complete defeat of the Axis cost them half a million men killed or taken prisoner in the whole campaign. Total Allied casualties were 70,000 men killed, missing, and wounded.

Among the high-ranking officers captured in the final days of the fighting was German General Von Arnim. Some of Eisenhower's aides thought that Ike should let Von Arnim visit him as a mark of courtesy. Eisenhower did not think so. The only Axis generals he was interested in, Ike said, were those the Allies had not yet taken prisoner. Eisenhower kept his word. He did not speak to a German general until the surrender terms were signed in 1945 at Reims, France.

The Mediterranean had now been cleared for Allied shipping, and the way lay open for "Operation Husky," the invasion of Sicily which had been decided upon by Allied leaders at a meeting of President Roosevelt, Winston Churchill, and the Combined Chiefs of Staff in Casablanca during the middle of the Tunisian campaign.

The Casablanca conference was held between January 14 and January 24, 1943. Roosevelt was the first President since Abraham Lincoln to visit a combat theater. Lincoln had done so more than three-quarters of a century earlier, during the Civil War. No other President had ever left the United States during a war.

While he was in Africa, Roosevelt managed to find time to visit with General Mark Clark and the American Fifth Army. The G.I.'s, who did not know that the high-level Casablanca conference was being held, were startled when their Commander-in-Chief suddenly joined them at a field mess for chow. The good-natured "F.D.R." chatted with a number of the surprised enlisted men as they ate.

The words of another Civil War leader, General Ulysses S. Grant, prompted President Roosevelt to tell the press at the end of the Casablanca meeting that the Allies would accept nothing less than "unconditional surrender" from the Axis. (Grant had demanded the unconditional surrender of Fort Donelson in Tennessee in 1862.) Churchill agreed with F.D.R.'s statement. A few months earlier the two Allied leaders might not have been so sure of the war's outcome. Now, however, the tide of victory was running for the Allies. The Russians had scored an epic victory at Stalingrad. The United States and Great Britain had swept the Axis from Africa. And halfway around the world in the Pacific theater of war, American arms were winning a stirring victory against the Japanese in the Battle of Guadalcanal in the Solomon Islands.

Eight

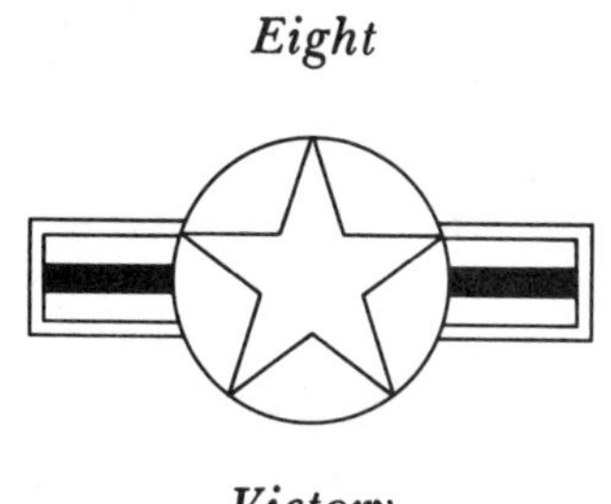

Victory on the Road to Tokyo

The battle for Guadalcanal was a nightmare for American land, sea, and air forces that lasted for six dark and terrible months. Out of this nightmare, however, grew the bright dawn of victory over the Japanese in the Pacific.

After the Japanese had received what President Roosevelt described as a "bloody nose" at Midway Island, they decided to risk no more fights in the mid-Pacific area. Instead they increased their efforts to isolate Australia. To do this they needed to complete their conquest of New Guinea and the Solomon Islands. The key to the control of the Solomons was Guadalcanal, and the Japanese had already landed some forces there and at Tulagi early in 1942.

On July 4 Admiral Ernest King received word that the Japanese were building an airfield on Guadalcanal. King knew that if the Japanese could use Guadalcanal as a stationary "aircraft carrier," they could easily cut the Allied lifeline to Australia. He immediately ordered Admiral Chester W. Nimitz, commander of the Pacific, to start "Operation Watchtower."

Watchtower was the American plan to seize the Solomons and eventually Rabaul on New Britain where the Japanese already had an important air and naval base. New Britain lay between the Solomons and New Guinea. Watchtower was not only the first American amphibious operation in the Pacific theater during World War II, but it was also the first such American operation since the Spanish-American War.

At dawn on August 7, 1942, the First Marine Division and parts of the Second Marine Division under General Alexander Vandegrift swarmed ashore on Guadalcanal and several nearby islands. Even before they landed, the Marines were aware of the foul, dank jungle smell coming from the rain forest of Guadalcanal — a rotten, swampy odor that they would remember for long months after the campaign was over.

The Marines met fierce resistance on small Gavatu Island. Here the Japanese defenders were loyal to their *bushido* code that made death in battle sacred. They died to the last man. Nevertheless, Gavatu was soon captured. Resistance elsewhere was slight. The unfinished air field on Guadalcanal was seized by late afternoon. It was renamed Henderson Field after Major Loften R. Henderson, a Marine flyer who had been killed at Midway. Tiny Tulagi Island with its fine harbor fell the next day.

The invasion of Guadalcanal had gone so smoothly that the Marines sat around cracking coconuts with their bayonets and wondering what was wrong. Where were the famous jungle-fighting Japanese who had fought so savagely in the Philippines and elsewhere? The Marines and the men aboard the warships that stood offshore to guard Guadalcanal did not have long to wait for the answer to their question.

The Japanese high command had been completely surprised by the invasion, but they reacted quickly. The Japanese Navy, aided by aircraft from Rabaul, was ordered to attack the Allied warships guarding Guadalcanal near Savo Island. In this battle on August 9, the United States Navy suffered one of its worst defeats. The Japanese quickly sank the American cruisers *Vincennes, Quincy,* and *Astoria* and the Australian cruiser *Canberra.* More than 1,000 Allied officers and men were lost and more than 700 were wounded, while the enemy suffered few casualties in either ships or men.

The Battle of Savo Island was just one of six major seafights that were fought off Guadalcanal during the next several months. Between the double row of islands that led to Guadalcanal was a long channel that became known as "The Slot." So many Japanese and American ships were sunk in the fierce struggle for control of the Slot that the area between Guadalcanal and Savo Island became known as "Ironbottom Sound."

After the Savo Island naval defeat the United States Marines on Guadalcanal were virtually isolated. The Japanese began to bring reinforcements to Guadalcanal via destroyers and troop transports. The Marines called this movement of enemy men and supplies through the Slot "the Tokyo Express."

On shore the Marines now began a grim fight to defend Henderson Field. They were soon short of food and had to cut their meals to two and then only one a day. For a time they lived on rice and canned fish they had captured from the Japanese.

Meanwhile, air and sea battles raged above and around Guadalcanal as the Americans fought savagely to land their own reinforcements. Gradually more Marines were landed, and they slowly drove the Japanese back through the dense jungle. This fighting took place under almost impossible conditions. The Marines could see only a few feet ahead of them through the thick barbed-wire-like tangle of vines and saw grass. Hidden Japanese snipers and machine gunners had to be blasted out of this dense cover. In addition to the Japanese, the Marines had to fight the terrible tropical heat, hunger, thirst, jungle diseases, insects, and animals. There were ants whose stings were like live coals. Giant spiders, wasps, scorpions, leeches, rats, lizards, and snakes attacked the men day and night. Relentlessly the Marines moved forward a yard at a time.

As Henderson Field was secured, Marine fighter pilots began to use it as an air base. These flyers soon added their own stories of courage to those epics being written by their fellows. One of the pilots who landed at Guadalcanal in September 1942 was destined to shoot down twenty-six enemy planes and thus tie the aerial combat record of America's World War I ace, Captain Eddie Rickenbacker. This was Captain Joseph Foss of Sioux Falls, South Dakota.

Joe Foss led a squadron of fighter pilots called the Flying Circus. A farm boy himself, Foss divided his flyers into two groups which he called the "Farm Boys" and the "City Slickers." The two teams competed fiercely for victories against the Japanese. Foss encouraged the competition, but he also emphasized teamwork — just as Captain Eddie Rickenbacker had done with his Hat-in-the-Ring Squadron on the Western Front in World War I. Foss compared successful combat flying with a successful football offensive, pointing out to his men that not one of them could score

G.I. jungle fighters in the South Pacific. (*U.S. Army Photo*)

without the close cooperation of his fellow team members. The Farm Boys and the City Slickers learned their lessons well. Their squadron shot down 208 enemy planes, more than any other Marine squadron.

The Foss Flying Circus flew together until January 1943, by which time Guadalcanal was safely in American hands, and the flyers could be returned to the United States for a well-earned rest. After the war Congressional Medal of Honor winner Joseph Foss became the Governor of his home state, South Dakota, and then head of professional football's American League.

* * *

A remarkable coincidence took place in the Pacific not far from Guadalcanal while Joe Foss was starting to score his victories. A Flying Fortress carrying eight men made a forced landing at sea, and seven of the eight survivors were finally rescued, after floating helplessly for three weeks aboard rubber life rafts. One of those rescued was Captain Eddie Rickenbacker, the man whose World War I aerial combat record Foss was to tie in this war.

Between the two wars Eddie Rickenbacker had pioneered in commercial aviation, becoming an important airlines executive. He had also been a stout defender of Billy Mitchell in Mitchell's fight for a strong and independent air force. When World War II began Rickenbacker was too old for combat duty, but Air Force Chief Hap Arnold and Secretary of War Henry Stimson had asked him to visit Army Air Force units at home and abroad. The purpose of these visits was to compare Allied and enemy aircraft and to study aerial combat methods. In this role Rickenbacker had gone to England early in the fall of 1942, returning to Washington in October. After Ricken-

Captain Eddie Rickenbacker. (U.S. Army Photo)

backer had made his report, Secretary Stimson asked him to visit combat groups in the Pacific theater of war.

Rickenbacker headed for Hawaii in late October. From there he was to fly to Australia, New Guinea, and Guadalcanal. Rickenbacker and seven others took off from Hickam Field, Hawaii, on October 21, 1942. Somehow they missed their first island destination en route to Australia, and their Fortress soon ran out of fuel. The pilot skillfully set the ship down in the sea, and all eight men survived the landing. Although several of them were injured, they were all able to climb aboard rubber life rafts. Then began a valiant fight against odds that has seldom been equalled in the history of men against the sea.

The men had no water to drink. Their only food was four oranges. The water through which the rafts drifted was shark-infested. The men had no idea where they were and no means by which they could call for help. They had no protection from the blazing tropical sun during the day or the cold at night. Rickenbacker called upon every ounce of the courage and determination that had made him America's Ace of Aces in World War I. He knew that to survive this ordeal, he and the other men would have to stick together more closely than he and his fellow flyers had ever done on the Western Front. He encouraged them in every way he knew how to keep up their spirits. The men sang together. They talked, wept, and finally prayed together for strength and courage.

On their eighth day adrift, a sea gull lit on Rickenbacker's head. Rickenbacker knew their situation was so desperate he simply *had* to catch the gull. Slowly, patiently, Rickenbacker raised his hand toward the bird and with a final quick movement grasped it. Quickly he killed the bird and divided it among the men, saving just a few pieces to use for bait to catch fish with a string and a bent pin.

Catching the gull seemed to bring a change in the men's fortune. They were able to land a few fish, and later a rain storm supplied fresh water that enabled them to survive a few days longer.

On the thirteenth morning, however, Staff Sergeant Alexander Kaczmarczyk died. Rickenbacker led a brief prayer and the sergeant was buried at sea. The survivors passed the next several days in a state of semi-consciousness. Finally, on their twenty-first day at sea, they were spotted by a flying boat. A short time later, a seaplane piloted by Lieutenant W. F. Eadie landed near the rubber rafts and the ordeal was over.

In addition to Rickenbacker, the men who were rescued included Colonel Hans C. Adamson, Captain William T. Cherry, Lieutenant James C. Whittaker, Lieutenant John De Angelis, Sergeant James W. Reynolds, and Private John F. Bartek.

Later, when Captain Joe Foss tied Captain Eddie Rickenbacker's aerial victory record, Rickenbacker was one of the first to congratulate the heroic Marine fighter pilot.

* * *

Unfortunately, not all of the sea stories about the Guadalcanal campaign ended as happily as the Rickenbacker saga. A story with a tragic ending was that of the five Sullivan brothers — Albert, 20; Madison, 22; Joseph, 23; Francis, 26; and George, 29. The Sullivan brothers were from Waterloo, Iowa. They had joined the United States Navy to avenge the death of their boyhood friend, William Ball of Fredericksburg, Iowa, who had been killed at Pearl Harbor. When the Sullivans joined the Navy, they requested that they all be assigned to the same ship. Although this was against Navy policy, the request was granted and all five were assigned to the light cruiser *Juneau,* a ship serving with the Guadalcanal Pacific Task Force.

During October 1942 the struggle for Guadalcanal was so severe that the Allied high command considered evacuating the island. President Roosevelt insisted, however, that it be held at all costs. Admiral William "Bull" Halsey was named commander of the Guadalcanal Pacific Task Force. Halsey was grimly determined to defeat the Japanese fleet.

In mid-November Japanese battleships and other naval forces moved down the Slot to bombard Henderson Field. Halsey knew that if Henderson Field were knocked out, the Marine riflemen on Guadalcanal would be at the mercy of Japanese carrier planes. He ordered his task force to intercept the Japanese Tokyo Express in Ironbottom Sound. On Friday, November 13, there began the blazing Battle of Guadalcanal, one of the most savage sea fights in naval history.

The opening round of the battle was fought to a draw. The two opposing naval forces met in head-on engagement in the predawn hours. Within half an hour, fierce broadsides had sunk two U.S. light cruisers and four destroyers. The Japanese lost two destroyers and a battleship — the first Japanese battleship to be sunk by the United States. The *Juneau* was in the thick of this fighting, inflicting heavy damage on the enemy and escaping unharmed.

Both sides now limped away to lick their wounds and to get ready to renew the fight. By mid-day a reinforced Tokyo Express moved down the Slot, and the *Juneau* and other ships of the task force moved in to intercept it. Just off Savo Island the *Juneau* was suddenly struck by a series of torpedoes fired by a Japanese submarine. The mortally wounded light cruiser sank in a few minutes, drowning some 700 men among whom were the five Sullivan brothers.

At the moment, of course, no one could take time to note the tragic loss, since this was the opening salvo in the grim second round of a fight to the death that was to continue almost without let-up for the next twenty-four hours. Halsey threw every weapon he had into the fight, including battleships, aircraft carriers, cruisers, and destroyers. From Guadalcanal Captain Joe Foss' Flying Circus and hundreds of other Marine fighter pilots added their blazing guns to the attack. The Japanese fleet also roared into action with every ship and plane available. In addition, the Japanese continued to try to land more infantry troops on Guadalcanal.

This round, however, was not fought to a draw. The Japanese were defeated and driven off. Not only did they fail to bombard Henderson Field, but they also failed to reinforce their ground forces there. In addition, they lost a pair of battleships, several destroyers, a cruiser, a dozen troop transports and had half a dozen destroyers and several cruisers so severely damaged they had difficulty limping away from the scene of action. Besides the *Juneau,* the U.S. lost the cruiser *Atlanta* and four destroyers.

The United States had been on the defensive at Guadalcanal when this naval battle began. When it ended, the tables had been turned and the Japanese were on the run. There was one more sea fight in the area in late November, and here, too, the Japanese met defeat. On the island itself, Japanese resistance continued until February 1943. But before then the United States was able to control the waters around the island and thus land Army infantry troops to relieve the Marines, many of whom were more dead than alive. So difficult were some of the enemy to find, however, that the last Japanese on the island did not surrender until October 27, 1947 — two years after the war ended.

During the six months' struggle for Guadalcanal, the

United States Navy lost some two dozen major warships as well as an equal number of PT boats and other smaller craft. But it was not the loss in ships and planes and other equipment that would be long remembered. It was the men who had paid with their lives to pave the way to victory along the road to Tokyo. And high on the list of those remembered were the Sullivan brothers.

When word of their death reached the United States, many people were reminded of a similar instance during the Civil War. In 1864 President Abraham Lincoln had written to a Massachusetts mother, Mrs. Lydia Bixby, telling her he had learned that five of her sons had "died gloriously on the field of battle. I feel how weak and fruitless must be any word of mine which should attempt to beguile you from the grief of a loss so overwhelming. But I cannot refrain from tendering to you the consolation that you may find in the thanks of the republic they died to save."

President Roosevelt wrote a similar letter to the Sullivan brothers' parents, but an even more touching letter was written by the President's wife, Eleanor Roosevelt. Because she too had sons serving in this war, Mrs. Roosevelt could share a mother's feelings with Mrs. Sullivan. Mrs. Roosevelt's letter read:

"My dear Mrs. Sullivan:

You and your husband have given a lesson of great courage to the whole country, and in thinking of this war and what it means to all mothers of the country I shall keep the memory of your fortitude always in mind, as I hope other mothers with sons in the service will do.

It is heartening that parents who have suffered the loss you have can always find solace in your faith and your abiding love for our country."

In February 1943 President Roosevelt approved naming a destroyer then under construction the *Sullivan.* In April Mrs. Sullivan christened the ship named for her sons, and when the destroyer *Sullivan* went to sea later that same month, serving aboard her was Patrick Henry Sullivan, forty-three-year-old uncle of the five heroic boys who had given their lives for their country.

* * *

Using Guadalcanal as a base, American Army, Navy, and Air Force units now began advancing up the chain of Solomon Islands. Their goal was the Japanese air and naval base at Rabaul, New Britain. Leapfrogging through the islands in a series of highly successful amphibious operations, the U.S. forces established new bases and airfields as they advanced. By November 1943 they had reached the island of Bougainville, within easy air-striking distance of Rabaul just 235 miles away.

During the campaign in the Solomons, the officers and crew of PT boat 109 had a memorable experience. On the night of August 1, 1943, their craft was one of four PT boats that left Rendova to attack Japanese shipping. During the night's action, PT-109 was rammed and sunk by an enemy destroyer.

Although the boat commander was injured, he rallied his crew and urged them to swim to the safety of a tiny volcanic island some miles away. One crew member was too badly injured to swim. The skipper put him into a life jacket and then, gripping the jacket strap in his teeth, he towed the injured man toward shore. They were in the water almost sixteen hours.

Once ashore, the exhausted skipper scratched their location on a coconut shell and gave the message to a native to carry to Rendova. A week later they were rescued. For

A Flying Fortress on a mission over Gizo Island in the Solomons. Near here PT 109 Skipper John F. Kennedy had a narrow escape from death. (Navy Department Photo in the National Archives)

his heroic efforts the PT-109 pilot was awarded the Navy and Marine Corps Medal and the Purple Heart. He did not get his greatest award, however, until November 1960, when former Navy Lieutenant j/g John F. Kennedy was elected the thirty-fifth President of the United States.

* * *

Meanwhile, in Australia General MacArthur was still determined to return to the Philippines. His best route, he believed, was along the northern shores of New Guinea. Thus MacArthur's offensive and the Solomons' offensive developed into a two-pronged attack on Rabaul. Instead of attempting to capture Rabaul, however, it was decided to attack by air and then isolate it by simply going around it and cutting off all Japanese air and sea supply routes to the vital enemy base. This was accomplished in late 1943 and early 1944 when MacArthur's forces landed in the Admiralty Islands. More than 100,000 Japanese troops were thus isolated, in effect neutralized, at Rabaul.

This method of bypassing enemy strongpoints and moving on to less strongly held islands of resistance was used against the Japanese in the southwest and central Pacific during the rest of the war. Costly frontal assaults were avoided whenever possible, and strongly held islands were isolated and then neutralized by powerful air attacks. Control of the air was, of course, essential to this type of operation. No amphibious landing could be successful unless enemy planes could be driven from the skies. The Japanese Air Force fought back fanatically, but unsuccessfully, against General George C. Kenney's Fifth Air Force and General Nathan F. Twining's Thirteenth Air Force in the New Guinea and Solomon Islands campaigns. Time and again, however, Kenney's and Twining's flyers shot down so many Japanese planes that they called combat engagements "turkey shoots."

Army flyers from Henderson Field scored their most important victory in mid-April 1943 when a squadron of twin-boomed P-38 Lightnings ambushed a flight of Japanese Zeros escorting a bomber carrying Admiral Isoroku Yamamoto to Bougainville. In the fierce aerial dogfight that followed between the P-38's and the Zeros, two American planes were lost, but the enemy admiral's plane was shot into the sea. The man who had planned the Pearl Harbor attack and who had said he would dictate peace terms in the White House was thus prevented from keeping his promise.

Control of the air was also to prove the key to victory in Western Europe. An invasion of France was now being planned, but before such an invasion could take place Germany's *Luftwaffe* would have to be driven from the skies. Right now this looked like an almost impossible task. In fact the Eighth Air Force bomber command was losing planes at such a crippling rate that a great strategic decision was facing the planners of the air war over Europe.

Nine

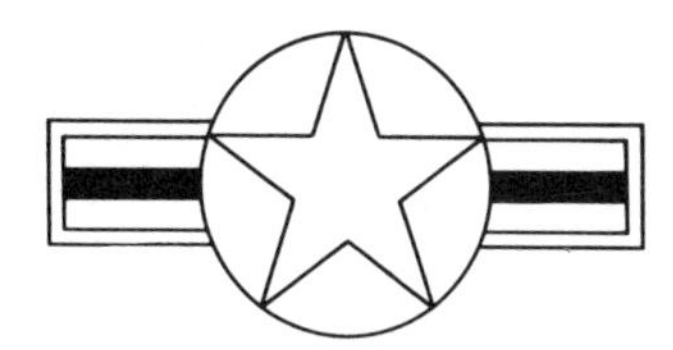

The Assault upon Fortress Europe

"Well, Ike, it looks like you're going to be in command of Operation Overlord," President Franklin Roosevelt said.

For a moment General Dwight Eisenhower was stunned. He had expected either a British general or United States Chief of Staff George Marshall to be placed in over-all charge of the Allied invasion of France. Finally Ike did manage to say, "Mr. President, I realize that such an appointment involved difficult decisions. I hope you won't be disappointed."

The Commander-in-Chief patted Ike on the shoulder reassuringly. "I won't be," he said.

The meeting between President Roosevelt and General Eisenhower took place at Tunis in early December 1943, just after a Combined Chiefs of Staff conference in Cairo, Egypt. At the Cairo conference it had been agreed that the Mediterranean area would become a secondary theater of war and that the main assault on Hitler's *Festung Europa* (Fortresss Europe) would be made across the English Channel and through France. Some thought had been given to naming British General Alan Brooke supreme commander of Overlord. Then it was realized that American forces would outnumber the British in the operation, and it was agreed that an American general should be picked for the post.

Eisenhower had proved his ability as a skillful diplomat in handling the Allied North African campaign; he had also proved his ability as an outstanding military leader in the successful invasions of Sicily and Italy that followed.

Operation Husky had been launched by American and British forces against Sicily on July 10, 1943. Immediately preceding it, General Lewis Brereton's Ninth Air Force and General Jimmy Doolittle's Twelfth Air Force had conquered the Italian Mediterranean island of Pantelleria by intensive bombing. This was the first such conquest made by aerial bombardment alone.

Sicily was also softened up for invasion by Allied air raids. The American ground forces were led ashore by Generals George Patton, Omar Bradley, and Lucian Truscott. With Britain's Eighth Army advancing up the east coast of the island and the American forces cutting through its center and up the west coast, Messina was captured and the Sicilian campaign ended on August 17.

Meanwhile, as the war approached the Italian mainland, Italy had tried frantically to get out of the war. Benito Mussolini was forced to resign as Premier and put into prison on July 25. Marshal Pietro Badoglio was named in his place. Later Mussolini was rescued from prison by German paratroopers and taken to Milan, where he set up a temporary puppet government for northern Italy.

Early in September the British Eighth Army had jumped off on "Operation Avalanche," the invasion of the toe of the Italian boot. A few days later the American Fifth Army under General Mark Clark hit the beaches south of Naples at Salerno. On September 8 Badoglio's government surrendered the Italian Army, and the fleet was surrendered on September 11.

Although Italy had now been knocked out of the war, veteran German troops on the peninsula gave no sign of surrender. Their infantry and armor fought back savagely. Allied air and naval support finally enabled the American G.I.'s to break out of their Salerno beachhead in mid-September, and they soon met the Eighth Army advancing from the south. By early October Naples had been captured, but much bitter winter fighting lay ahead.

* * *

During this grim fighting up the Italian boot, the American G.I.'s and the British Tommies cemented the comradeship in battle that had had its beginnings in North Africa. It was not only Allied men, however, who had their friendship and bravery tested in the fires of combat in the Italian campaign. A heroic carrier pigeon also performed a remarkable feat of gallantry, for which he was later awarded the Dickin Medal — the animal world equivalent of the United States Congressional Medal of Honor or the British Victoria Cross.

The pigeon was called "G.I. Joe." Joe was a slate blue bird belonging to the United States Army Signal Corps but serving on temporary duty with the British Eighth Army. On the morning of October 18 the British Fifty-sixth Infantry Division was trying desperately to capture a heavily fortified German position at Colvi Vecchia. Wave after wave of Tommies had been broken by German machine guns and mortars. Finally, the British officer in command sent back a request for the American Twelfth Air Force to bombard the enemy-held position. After the re-

"G.I. Joe," the heroic pigeon that was given the animal world's highest award for carrying a message that saved the lives of a number of Allied troops. (U.S. Army Signal Corps Photo)

quest had been received, radio communications between the British and Americans broke down.

Moments later the British infantry made a final fierce attack on Colvi Vecchia and succeeded in capturing the town. Now, however, the commanding officer feared that his victorious men might become the accidental victims of the aerial bombardment that was to begin within half an hour. In such a short time it would be impossible to contact all of his troops and order them out of the town. Their lone carrier pigeon would have to fly a message back to headquarters cancelling the request for air support. G.I. Joe was hurriedly taken from his pen and the vital message was attached to his leg. Then he was tossed into the air. Despite enemy rifle fire and enemy and Allied shell fire, Joe headed straight as an arrow toward headquarters. His destination was more than twenty miles away. Unwaveringly he flew the distance in twenty minutes, arriving just as the Twelfth Air Force planes were preparing to take off for the target. Had the message arrived even a few minutes later, hundreds of British soldiers' lives would have been lost.

Joe was credited with the most outstanding flight made by a United States Army carrier pigeon in World War II. After the war he was flown from the United States to England in an Army plane to be awarded the British Dickin Medal in ceremonies held at the Tower of London. Photographers, newsreel men, and British Broadcasting Company commentators were present at the ceremonies. They were also reported in the London *Times,* and it was pointed out that this was the first time that the so-called Animals' Victoria Cross had ever been awarded to an animal or bird other than British.

* * *

When General Eisenhower returned to England to set up his Supreme Headquarters, Allied Expeditionary Forces (SHAEF) for the invasion of France, he took Jimmy Doolittle with him to replace Ira Eaker as commanding general of the Eighth Air Force. When Doolittle asked what his orders were, Ike said, "Destroy the *Luftwaffe.* If you can destroy it in the air, fine. If not, hunt out its airfields and aircraft factories and destroy the planes before they get into the air."

"Yes, sir," Doolittle said. He knew Ike's orders meant sending daylight air raids deep into the heart of Germany, and to date all such efforts had resulted in tragic losses.

No American bomber force had ever turned back from a mission — none would, during the entire war — but several groups were almost destroyed by the *Luftwaffe*.

From the time the Eighth Air Force first arrived in England, American and British commanders had disagreed about daylight aerial bombardment. The British had tried it early in the war but, after suffering crippling losses, they had turned to night bombing. Their giant Lancaster and Halifax bombers were designed for this purpose, carrying few machine guns and a maximum bomb load with which to "blanket" the target. The United States, however, had designed its B-17 Fortress and B-24 Liberator for daylight raids. The Fortress and Liberator each had tremendous fire power plus the remarkably accurate and secret Norden bombsight. This bombsight was valued so highly that it was removed from each plane after every mission and locked in a guarded supply room. Before each new mission the bombardier was accompanied by armed guards as he carried the Norden sight from the supply room to his plane. This secret bombsight was highly prized for good reason. With it American bombardiers had proved they could "drop a bomb in a pickle barrel." But "pickle barrel" or precision bombing had to be done in daylight.

Under General Eaker the Eighth Air Force had suffered few losses in its early raids on the continent, but on these early missions the bombers were given close fighter plane protection. As soon as they began to fly beyond the range of their own fighter escort, the Fortresses and Liberators were dealt staggering blows by the *Luftwaffe's* Messerschmitt Me-109's and Focke-Wulf FW 190's — two of the finest fighter planes ever built.

At the Casablanca meeting of the Combined Chiefs of Staff early in 1943 it had been at first decided to abandon daylight precision bombing. Then General Eaker had flown down from England and had a long talk with Win-

A formation of B-24 Liberators on a mission. (U.S. Air Force Photo)

A B-24, flying at smokestack height, bombs the Ploesti oil field. (U.S. Air Force Photo)

ston Churchill in an effort to convince the British Prime Minister that daylight bombardment had not been fully tested. Churchill seemed to be unconvinced until Eaker pointed out that with "around-the-clock bombing," that is with the British bombing Germany at night and the Americans during the day, Germany would have no rest. Churchill remained more or less unconvinced, but he agreed to give the experiment a further trial. He seemed particularly to like Eaker's "around-the-clock" phrase and used it in a public speech a few days later.

The answer to the problem of large losses in daylight raids was, of course, to furnish the Eighth Air Force with fighter planes that could accompany the bombers to the target and back. No such long-range fighter was available, however, until late in 1943. Nevertheless, the Eighth Air Force flew its daylight precision bombardment missions against Fortress Europe, taking its terrible losses in grim silence and biding its time.

The Ninth Air Force flying out of Africa had suffered similar losses. On August 1, 1943, it had sent 177 Liberators (some of which were borrowed from the Eighth Air Force) on a mission to bomb vital Axis oil refineries at Ploesti, Rumania. Fifty-four planes and more than 400 men were lost. Five of the survivors were awarded the Medal of Honor for this low-level mission which went in at smokestack height. The raid had been only partly successful, however.

On August 17, 1943, just one year after its bombers had first attacked the continent, the Eighth Air Force sent 376 Fortresses on missions from England into Germany against ballbearing and aircraft factories at Schweinfurt and Regensburg. Sixty American bombers and some 600 men were shot down. Both targets were accurately bombed, but the losses were so great that it began to look as if the Eighth Air Force might be wiped out.

In the midst of this aerial carnage, the American flyers managed somehow to keep their wry sense of humor. On the Schweinfurt raid two aerial gunners took along a milk can filled with liquid ice cream mix that they knew would freeze into ice cream during their long flight at high altitude. The can was punctured by several enemy machine-gun slugs, but the frozen mixture and the aerial gunners safely survived the mission. That night the gunners served ice cream "made over Germany" to the rest of their Fortress crew.

The Regensburg mission was called a "shuttle raid," because, after the target was hit, the Eighth Air Force planes flew on to Africa instead of returning directly to England. A few days later when the surviving planes were flown back to England, one crew brought with them a little African burro. The burro had to be equipped with an oxygen mask, but it made the trip safely and was promoted to sergeant by the crew and awarded the air medal.

"If he's going to be our mascot," the bomber pilot told his enlisted gunners, "the least you could do is make him an officer."

"We would," one of the sergeants said, "but we don't want him to run away."

General Eaker had continued to hope for fewer losses on unescorted heavy bomber raids into Germany. On Thursday, October 14, 1943, some 291 "Queens of Battle," as the crews called their beloved Fortresses, were once again sent to Schweinfurt. This "Black Thursday" mission went down in Air Force history as the most savage air battle ever fought. At the height of the battle few of the men who were still alive ever expected to get back to England. Hundreds did not. P-47 Thunderbolt fighter planes escorted the Fortresses as far as Aachen, Germany, on this mission, but the *Luftwaffe* waited just out of fighter range to pounce on the bomber formations. For this all-day battle the *Luftwaffe* put in the air virtually every plane of every kind that it had. A number of crack fighter squadrons and pilots had also been recalled from the Russian front. The planes the Germans used to attack the Fortresses included single-engine Messerschmitts, Focke-Wulfs, and Heinkels, as well as twin-engine Messerschmitts and rocket-firing Junkers. In addition, they threw into the battle planes that had never been designed as high altitude fighters, including the old-fashioned Stukas whose wheels could not be retracted. Even four-engine Heinkel bombers attacked the gallant Schweinfurt-bound Queens with rockets and cannons.

The *Luftwaffe* also used new methods of attack in this battle. The single-engine planes would come barrel-rolling through the Fortress formations head-on, while the twin-engine planes attacked with rockets from the side. Parachutes carrying aerial bombs were also dropped among the B-17's. As soon as a formation gave signs of spreading out, swarms of German fighters would gang up on an individual Fortress and destroy it. The Germans used this method of killing off one plane at a time all the way into the target and then back out again. Fortress gunners fired their machine guns until the barrels threatened to melt, and before the raid was over there was a serious shortage of ammunition. Men, parts of planes, parachutes and all kinds of debris hurtled through the air past the smoke-blinded Fortress crews — but they flew relentlessly toward their target.

In this battle, as in all of the other battles of the air offensive in Western Europe, the Fortresses themselves, gallant Queens of the skies, seemed to have a stubborn life of their own. Hit time and again by machine-gun fire, rockets, cannon fire, the Queens flew on when often the men inside them did not know what was keeping them in the air. One Fortress suffered a head-on collision with a German fighter plane that all but ripped the bomber in half and caused the fighter to explode. The only thing that seemed to be connecting the Queen's tail section to the fore part of the fuselage was the plane's flooring, yet it flew on, dropped its bombs, and fought its way out of Germany and back to England.

Of the 291 Fortresses that were sent on the mission, 229 successfully attacked Schweinfurt, inflicting severe damage on the ballbearing plants and thus cutting down on German aircraft production. The Eighth Air Force Bomber Command lost 60 Fortresses and 600 men. Many other planes were severely damaged and many other men were severely wounded.

This second Schweinfurt raid proved unbearably costly to the Eighth Air Force. Mercifully, bad weather settled over the European continent for the next several months, just as it had in 1942. No more raids deep into Germany could now be run. Even if there had been good weather, however, it is doubtful whether Germany would have been attacked by daylight again until long-range fighter escort planes were available.

The American air crews in England accepted the fact that their ships were "weathered in" as a reprieve from death. They knew they had to fly twenty-five missions before they would be relieved from combat duty and returned to the United States. Their losses to date, however, had averaged almost five per cent per mission. This meant that by the end of twenty-five missions the entire force with which they first went into combat could be destroyed. So the crews now settled back to "sweat out" yet one more British winter. They loafed in their "huts" (barracks), or at the Red Cross "Aero Club." Sometimes they rode bicycles on a "short mission" into the local village or took a weekend pass into London. Many of them dated English girls and a number of these romances resulted in mar-

Many American airmen called the Flying Fortress "the greatest bomber ever built." This picture shows why. Although a collision with a German fighter plane all but cut this "Queen of Battle" in half, the pilot managed to fly the battered bomber back to its base. (U.S. Air Force Photo)

riages. Most of the men, however, had wives or sweethearts at home, and writing and receiving letters became the most important part of the day. Daily mail call always resulted in a stampede as the men rushed to get their letters from home.

Because mail was so important to morale, everything possible was done to speed its delivery. One of the methods used was the V-mail service. V-mail letters were written on a special form, the forms were photographed on 16-mm. film, and the film was flown to overseas processing stations. There enlarged prints were made from the microfilm, and these "V-letters" were delivered to the addressees.

The exact origin of the V-mail service is unknown. The British used a similar method called an "Airgraph" beginning in May 1941. The first American V-mail film of 212 letters was flown from New York to London on June 22, 1942. This was only a partially filled roll, however. A full roll held as many as 1,600 letters. Microfilm of 150,000 letters weighed about forty-five pounds and could be carried in a single mail sack. The same number of letters in their original form filled thirty-seven mail sacks. More than one and a half billion V-mail letters were sent and received by the Armed Forces overseas during World War II.

An early forerunner of modern wartime V-mail was used during the siege of Paris in the Franco-Prussian War of 1870-71 when the Prussians completely surrounded the French capital. To get mail into the city a carrier pigeon postal service was organized in the free areas of France. As a part of this service a special photography studio was set up at Tours. Here messages were placed on a large board, photographed, and then greatly reduced in size. The film was then rolled up and inserted in a capsule that was fastened to the leg of a carrier pigeon. Each Paris-bound bird could carry several thousand brief messages in a single flight. In Paris the films were projected onto a screen and then copied by hand for delivery to the addressees.

As soon as there was a break in the weather, the men of the Eighth Air Force began to fly missions again. Some of these were "milk runs" — short flights against weakly defended targets in France — but many were dangerous precision attacks against such targets as well-defended enemy submarine pens. By adding extra "belly" fuel tanks to the P-47 Thunderbolts and twin-fuselaged P-38's, the planes' range was increased enough to enable them to fly medium-range escort missions. But the fighter planes could give the bombers no protection against the murderous "flak" from enemy anti-aircraft guns, and Fortresses and Liberators and their crews continued to be shot down over the continent.

* * *

Not all of the men who were shot down were killed, of course. And not all of those who survived by bailing out of their stricken ships were taken prisoner. The French resistance and underground forces succeeded in rescuing many Allied flyers who parachuted to earth in occupied Europe. These escapees were often hidden in French homes — sometimes for months — and then passed along from house to house until they reached Spain. Spain was technically a neutral country in the war, but allowed Allied airmen who reached Spanish soil to be returned to England.

Several thousand American airmen shot down in France were spirited out of the country by this underground system. One woman, Mrs. Gunocente Lauro, who lived in the village of Lamorlaye near Chantilly, hid and took care of more than a hundred escapees during the course of the war. She hid one pilot, a badly wounded American major, in her house for two months until he was well enough to travel.

The Germans who occupied Lamorlaye did not know it, but Mrs. Lauro was an English woman. Several years before the war, while vacationing in Italy, she had met and married Gunocente, who made his living training horses. The Lauros had one child, a daughter who was three years old when the war started. During the same week that Germany occupied northern France early in the war Gunocente had brought some horses to run in the annual racing meet at Chantilly. The Germans made Gunocente go to work for them as a groom in the cavalry stables in Chantilly. Since he was an Italian and an Axis ally, however, they allowed him to bring his wife and child from Italy to live in Lamorlaye. They also allowed the Lauro family a considerable amount of freedom without watching them closely.

Mrs. Lauro took advantage of the fact that the Germans trusted her and her husband. She never spoke a word of English in the presence of the Germans. She also let it be known among the local members of the French resistance that she was on their side, and soon the Lauro home became a station on the underground network for shuttling escaping Allied airmen into Spain. She did this work at great risk to herself and her family. If she had been caught, the Lauro family would have been shot. Her risks were increased by the fact that the German commanding officer in Lamorlaye came to the Lauro home each evening to play chess with Gunocente. On many such evenings an escaping flyer would be hiding in the bedroom just a few yards away from the German colonel sitting in the kitchen, and the doorway between the two rooms would be open except for a thick cloth curtain. On all of the evenings when the American major was in the house recovering from his severe wounds Mrs. Lauro made her little daughter stay in the bedroom with him when the German colonel came to play chess with her husband.

"In this way," she later explained to a member of the United States counterintelligence service, "if the major cried out from his wounds I could immediately say it was my daughter making the sound."

"Did this ever happen?" she was asked.

"Yes," she said, smiling, "but my little girl was quite bright and alert. She immediately ran into the kitchen to tell us she had been asleep and had been awakened by a bad dream. The German colonel was quite taken in by it."

Mrs. Lauro did not confine her resistance efforts to rescuing Allied flyers. One time she learned that a whole railroad box car filled with potatoes from Poland had been shipped into Chantilly for the German officers' mess hall. She made the local druggist give her several large bottles of sulfuric acid and that night she stole into the freight yard and dumped the poison all over the potatoes.

"Weren't you ever afraid for your life in doing all of this?" she was asked.

Mrs. Lauro laughed. "I found it quite exciting," she said.

* * *

Early in 1944, shortly after General Jimmy Doolittle took command of the Eighth Air Force, a great new American fighter plane was just beginning to arrive in the European theater in sufficient numbers to make large-scale daylight raids into Germany possible. This was the P-51 Mustang. Originally it had a range of about 600 miles. Soon, however, it was equipped with extra gas tanks, and its range leaped to 2,000 miles. The crews of the Fortresses and Liberators came to love this little ship so much they called it "little friend" and "little brother." The Mustang

Flying Fortresses and their fighter escort weave vapor trails in the sky on the way to bomb Berlin. (U.S. Air Force Photo)

made it possible for Doolittle's bombers to stage a series of raids deep in the heart of Germany during what was called "Big Week," and even to attack the capital of Germany itself, "Big B," or Berlin.

The British R.A.F. had, of course, been staging thousand-plane night bomber raids for some months. They had set Cologne and Hamburg aflame so that fires in those cities raged for days. Now, however, it also became possible for the Eighth Air Force to stage similar mass raids by day, and "around-the-clock bombing" became a reality.

Striking at Berlin and the heart of Germany gave particular satisfaction to the Eighth Bomber Command. Not only did it give them an opportunity to avenge such losses as those suffered at Schweinfurt, but it also made *Luftwaffe* leader Hermann Goering eat his words.

When the Eighth Air Force had first appeared in Europe, Goering was quoted as saying, "If the Americans ever bomb Berlin, you can call me Meyer." Ground crews loading the bombs into the first Fortresses that were to fly to Berlin chalked a message on the bombs that read, "Where's Meyer?"

"Meyer" Goering had also scoffed, "All the Americans can make is razor blades and refrigerators." Now "Meyer" was being shown that Americans could also manufacture an air force that could drive the vaunted *Luftwaffe* from the skies. In fact so well did the American and British Air Forces accomplish this job that the Allies were to have absolute command of the air during the invasion of Normandy that was now just a few months away.

"Without complete command of the air," General Eisenhower said, "the invasion of France would have been impossible. As it was, resistance from the *Luftwaffe* on D-Day was almost nonexistent."

Ten

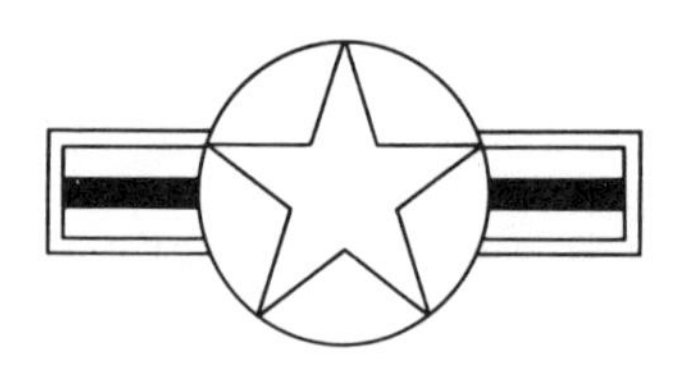

D-Day in Normandy

On a stormy Sunday night in early June 1944 General Dwight Eisenhower met with the other members of his high command at Southwick House near Portsmouth in southern England. The purpose of the meeting was to decide whether or not orders should be given for the Allied invasion of France to begin. This morning, June 4, Operation Overlord had already been postponed for a day. Now, judging by the way the wind and rain were beating against the house, it might have to be postponed indefinitely. Such a decision, Ike knew, could mean failure. Ships and planes, sailors, airmen, infantrymen, and paratroopers were like cocked guns — aimed and ready. They could not be kept on such an alert indefinitely.

Captain J. N. Stagg, R.A.F. weather officer, now entered

the library where the meeting was being held. Every officer in the room hung on Stagg's words as he gave the weather prediction: despite the present storm, it looked like there would be clearing weather tomorrow that would hold through Tuesday morning, June 6.

Although he knew he alone must make the final decision, Ike nevertheless asked each of the other officers his opinion. British Air Marshals Leigh-Mallory and Tedder thought that the heavy clouds might make it impossible for the heavy and medium bombers to hit their targets.

General Walter Bedell Smith, Ike's chief of staff, thought the order to attack should be given.

"Monty?" Ike asked General Bernard Montgomery. The famed commander of the British Eighth Army was now in over-all command of the Allied ground forces for Overlord.

"I say go!" Montgomery said firmly.

There was now general discussion. British Admiral Bertram Ramsay, commander of the Allied sea forces, and Admiral Alan Kirk, commander of the U.S. naval units, insisted a decision one way or another had to be reached soon or their ships would not be able to sail in time.

Finally General Eisenhower interrupted. "All right," he said, "the question is how long can we keep our men dangling at the end of a limb?"

There was complete silence in the room.

"I'm positive we must give the order for the attack to begin," Ike said quietly. Then he added, "We'll go."

Overlord, the long-awaited invasion of Nazi-held France, was under way.

After long and careful study the beaches of Normandy between Le Havre and Cherbourg had been chosen for the invasion. The Germans were completely fooled by this

Ike talking with paratroopers just before they boarded their plane to take part in the invasion of Hitler's Fortress Europe. (U.S. Army Photo)

choice for the Allied assault. They expected landings at Calais in the Pas de Calais region. The Allies had neatly tricked them into believing this.

For weeks and months before the invasion, at least two planes were sent to bomb targets in the Pas de Calais area every time one was sent to bomb targets behind the landing beaches. In addition, General George Patton was used as a decoy. He was allowed to maneuver his tanks in the open in English fields just opposite Calais. Occasional German photo reconnaisance planes were allowed to fly in and take pictures of Patton's maneuvers so that *Luftwaffe* intelligence officers would have proof that Calais was the place the Allies were planning to attack. The Germans remembered Patton's slashing successes in North Africa and Sicily, so they were ready to believe he would spearhead the invasion of Normandy.

Eisenhower planned to use Patton all right — but not until some time after the invasion. Once the beaches were secured, Eisenhower regarded Patton as the ideal commander to lead the Third Army in an armored attack to break through the German defense lines.

Ike had not had an easy time convincing General Marshall and other members of the high command that Patton should play a key role in the invasion or afterwards. In Italy the high-strung, outspoken Third Army commander had caused an uproar by slapping a hospitalized G.I. who was recovering from a bad case of battle fatigue. Patton thought only wounded men should be in the hospital. Later he apologized publicly for the incident.

In England, Patton, thinking he was speaking "off-the-record," made a statement to the effect that he thought it would be a good idea for the United States and England to get together after the war and rule the world. This time Ike asked Patton for a written report of the incident and then reprimanded him. When Patton apologized profusely and offered to resign, Ike said:

"You're not going to get out of it that easily. You owe us some victories, George, and I'm going to keep you around to see that you get them for us."

General Marshall also spoke to Patton. He did it indirectly, however, through a public relations officer. When the officer, a captain, arrived at Patton's headquarters, Patton asked him sharply what he wanted.

The captain looked Patton straight in the eye and said, "Sir, General Marshall says you should shut up!"

Patton blinked. Then he grinned. "Captain, I think you and I are going to get along all right." The public relations captain served with Patton during the remainder of the campaign in Europe.

Another reason the Germans did not think the Allies would attack across the Normandy beaches was because there were no ports in the area. Here again the Allies fooled them by bringing along two portable harbors. It was originally planned to call these portable harbors "Churchills" because the Prime Minister had thought of them as far back as World War I when he was the First Lord of the Admiralty. Instead they were called "Mulberries" for the mulberry bushes that cover the Normandy countryside and form its hedgerows. To supply the invasion forces with gasoline, a portable pipeline was strung along the floor of the English Channel. This was called "PLUTO," for "Pipeline Under the Ocean."

Even when the actual landings began, the Germans could not believe that this was D-Day. They thought the sea was too rough for landing craft and other small vessels to attempt the assault. When the Germans began to react, their reactions came almost too late. One of the first things they called for, of course, was the *Luftwaffe* to help drive off the invaders. The Royal Air Force and the United States Air Force had done a superb job of knocking out the *Luftwaffe*. Only a slim handful of fighter planes rose to defend Normandy on D-Day as more than a thousand Eighth Air Force heavy bombers smashed at the beach defenses.

The United States Ninth Air Force had also played a key role in paving the way for the landings. In October 1943 General Brereton's Ninth Air Force had been transferred from Africa to England, and its heavy bombers were made a part of the United States Strategic Air Force under General Carl Spaatz. The Ninth, which was later commanded by General Hoyt Vandenberg, flew fighter planes, medium and attack or fighter bombers, and troop carrier planes from its new bases in England.

The job of the medium and fighter bombers was to knock out enemy airfields, bridges, motor transport, railroad yards and railroad lines as well as coastal gun positions. In the week before D-Day alone, the Ninth flew about 40,000 sorties (a sortie was one plane flying one combat mission), or more than 5,000 a day. These raids almost completely stopped all enemy troop and supply movement from the interior of France to the Channel coast. The Ninth's troop carrier planes were used to tow gliders carrying airborne infantry and to drop paratroopers into France for the invasion.

British paratroopers and members of the U.S. 82nd and 101st Airborne Divisions were the first men ashore on Tuesday morning, June 6, 1944. They were dropped behind the enemy lines at two a.m. at points ranging from Cherbourg to Caen. General Matthew Ridgway, commander of the 82nd, and General Maxwell Taylor, commander of the 101st, personally led their men into battle. Their orders were to capture key strongpoints, destroy bridges, knock out vital gun positions, and protect the Allied right flank. Although they were bent on deadly missions of destruction, the airborne infantrymen used a children's toy as an assembly signal once they had landed. This was a small tin "cricket," and its thin chirping sound could be heard across the silent and dark Normandy countryside after the scattered paratroopers had landed and began to gather into combat units to set about their grim morning's mission.

Immediately after an intense naval bombardment from hundreds of battleships, the first assault waves of Allied seaborne infantrymen began landing at 6:30 a.m. The British and Canadian forces under General Miles Dempsey and the American forces under General Omar Bradley struck at five points along fifty miles of coast line. The British and Canadian beaches were named "Sword," "Juno," and "Gold." The American beaches were called "Omaha" and "Utah." More than 4,500 ships carrying more than 200,000 men made up the invasion armada for this greatest amphibious attack in history.

Despite the air and naval bombardment, the first wave of men to storm ashore found most of the German beach defenses intact. These included giant iron obstacles sunk beneath the water and barbed wire strung along the shore. Floating mines also threatened the landing craft. Once they were out of their landing craft, the men found the beaches were heavily mined. Concrete gun emplacements were arranged so the German machine gunners inside them had a clear field of fire along the landing areas. Anti-tank walls, mine fields, and deep ditches guarded all the exits from the beaches.

In the British and Canadian sectors and in the American sector at Utah beach the landings went according to plan. There was severe opposition in several places, but it was quickly overcome. The U.S. Fourth Division at Utah

Normandy beach landings. (U.S. Army Photo)

met only light resistance and by nightfall had driven inland for six miles, meeting up with General Taylor's airborne troops.

At Omaha beach, however, it was a different story. Here a crack German division was encountered almost by accident. It had been on training maneuvers in the area and was immediately thrown into action against the American First and Twenty-ninth Divisions attempting landings at Omaha. For five dreadful hours G.I.'s of the First and Twenty-ninth were pinned to a few yards of beach shingle beneath the withering German fire, hanging on almost literally by their finger nails. So desperate did the situation become that some thought was given to landing additional Omaha troops at nearby Gold beach.

The men who came ashore at Omaha, and lived to tell the tale, never forgot these desperate hours. As soon as their landing craft touched down, a hail of rifle and machine-gun fire, mortar and artillery shells exploded around them. The instant the landing craft ramps were lowered, the men met a wall of machine-gun fire. Some landing craft ground to a halt too far from the beach, and many men drowned as they leaped into the deep water and were dragged under by their heavy packs.

Nevertheless, demolition men moved into the raging fire to try and clear a way through the thorn-steel barbed wire and beach obstacles. Some of these obstacles were steel beams driven into the sand. Others were made up of several I-beams set together at right angles. Many had mines wired on top of them. Other beams had razor-sharp edges. There were also mined wooden logs and mines hidden in blocks of cement.

As the demolition men worked desperately to fix their charges and blow gaps in the wire, some infantrymen tried to take cover behind the obstacles themselves. This was

The German S-mine delayed the Allied advance in the Mediterranean and European theaters of war. G.I.'s called it the "Bouncing Betty" because when it was stepped on it shot several feet into the air before scattering hundreds of deadly steel balls in all directions. (U.S. Army Photo)

fatal. It was only a matter of time before the men who remained on the beach shingle were killed. Officers and noncoms knew this, and they did their best to "dig the men out" and lead them inland. Here, as in every battle, leadership played a vital role.

In one area a lieutenant and a sergeant rose in the face of enemy fire and strolled leisurely ahead to inspect the barbed wire that blocked their path. Overhead the German 88's were making their fearful bzz-YOO! bzz-YOO! sound followed by a boom-boom-BLANG! boom-boom-BLANG as they hit. The wicked ku-BLAM! ku-BLAM! of mortar fire was all around them, and incessantly the machine-gun and small arms fire beat a background snare drum roll for the heavy base drum beat of the artillery.

In spite of the death and destruction around them, the sergeant and lieutenant walked slowly back to their men lying face down on the beach at the water's edge. Hands on hips, the lieutenant said sharply, "Are you going to lie there and get killed, or get up and do something about it?" The men still refused to move. The sergeant and lieutenant then blew the wire, and the men advanced inland.

Another lieutenant crawled along on his hands and knees probing for mines with a hunting knife as he led his men forward.

At another spot on Omaha beach Colonel George Taylor found his men huddled at the water's edge, where they were rapidly being cut down by enemy fire.

"Two kinds of people are staying on this beach," Colonel Taylor shouted at them, "the dead and those who are going to die. Now let's get the blazes out of here!"

Moments later the men charged with Colonel Taylor through gaps in the wire and drove back the enemy.

Reinforcements continued to be landed and by nightfall the landings on Omaha beach as well as elsewhere were secured. Word was flashed to General Eisenhower and an anxiously waiting world that the Allied forces were firmly established in France. The long-awaited Second Front had become a reality. On this same day twenty-six years earlier, American fighting men had begun another epic battle against the Germans in France, the Battle of Belleau Wood in World War I which began on June 6, 1918. The brave old doughboys from that earlier war could be

G.I.'s going ashore on the Normandy beaches. (U.S. Army Photo)

proud of the equally heroic young G.I.'s and the feats of arms they performed this day on the beaches of Normandy.

With the "crust" of the German defense broken, it would be only a matter of days before the beaches were so firmly occupied that the Combined Chiefs of Staff themselves could visit the combat area. Many G.I.'s were startled on June 12 suddenly to see General Marshall, General Arnold, and Admiral King being escorted by General Eisenhower on a tour of the beaches.

"This place *must* be safe now," one G.I. commented, "if that kind of brass can be here!"

Safety had been bought at a high price, however. D-Day casualties amounted to more than 10,000 Allied men. U.S. losses were more than 6,000 killed and wounded. The British suffered about 2,500 total casualities, and the Canadians about 1,000.

At least one high-ranking German officer had now begun to see the handwriting on the wall. When asked by the German high command shortly after the D-Day landings what defensive measures should be taken, Field Marshal Gerd von Rundstedt snapped, "Make peace, you fools!"

But Adolf Hitler still had an ace up his sleeve. This was the "buzz bomb."

On the very day the Combined Chiefs were visiting the beaches, the first German buzz bomb, the V-1, struck London. The V-1 was a small pilotless aircraft that carried a large bomb load. Its steering mechanism was preset at take-off and the fiendish device exploded on landing.

Still later, in August, the Germans launched the V-2 against England. This was a high flying rocket that carried explosives. The V-1 could be seen, intercepted, and shot down. The V-2, however, traveled so high and fast that it struck without warning.

Normandy beach two days after the landings. (U.S. Army Photo)

The Allied high command had been aware for some time that the Germans were working on this secret device. One of the German experimental stations was at Peenemünde on the Baltic Sea, and numerous air raids had been sent against this installation. When launching ramps for the V-1 began to appear along the Channel coast, aerial bombardment was also used against them.

Once the V-1 and V-2 attacks began, another method of attack was tried to destroy their launching sites. This was an attempt to send a radio-controlled "drone" airplane packed with high explosives to dive directly into the landing sites and destroy them. A human pilot had to take off in these drone airplanes, however, and then aim the explosive-filled ship toward the continent. The pilot also had to set the mechanism of the drone so a "mother" ship could guide the drone the rest of the way to the target. Once this was done, the pilot was supposed to bail out of the drone and parachute to safety.

Several pilots were killed while the Allies tried desperately to perfect this drone-and-mother-ship device. For some unknown reason the explosive-filled drones frequently exploded in mid-air at the exact moment when the pilot set the controls for the mother ship to take over. The experiment was finally abandoned, but before it was abandoned one of the drone pilots who was killed was Navy Lieutenant Joseph Kennedy, Jr., older brother of John Kennedy, future President of the United States. Joe Kennedy was posthumously awarded the Navy Cross for valor. Later a destroyer was named for him.

Eventually the buzz bombs and rocket bombs were brought under control through the combined efforts of fighter pilots shooting down the V-1's and Allied infantry capturing the V-1 and V-2 launching sites. Before this was accomplished, more than 16,000 V-1's and 14,000 V-2's rained death and destruction upon England.

* * *

For several weeks after the successful Normandy invasion the Allies fought fiercely to enlarge their beachhead. Their efforts were seriously threatened on June 19 when the worst storm in half a century swept down the English Channel. For several days communications between the Allied armies in France and SHAEF headquarters in England were cut off. No reinforcements or supplies could be sent to France, and offensive fighting ground to a halt. One of the two Mulberries — the one on Omaha beach — was destroyed, and the other in the British sector was damaged. Nevertheless, as soon as the storm ended the build-up of men and supplies began again. By the end of the month Cherbourg was captured by General Lawton Collins' VII Corps and U.S. engineers went to work repairing its docks and clearing its harbor so it could be used as a port.

In battling their way out of the beachhead the G.I.'s had their first bitter experience with hedgerow fighting. The Normandy hedgerows made ideal defense positions for the Germans. At fifty-yard intervals double rows of dirt mounds surrounded all of the Normandy farm pastures. Planted along these mounds were thick hedges of mulberry and other trees whose roots formed a thick tangled matting in the earth. Infantrymen found it almost impossible to get through these hedgerows, behind which German machine-gunners and riflemen could hide in perfect safety. When American tanks tried to climb the earth mounds they exposed their vulnerable bellies to German anti-tank guns.

General Omar Bradley asked all of his men for suggestions on how to conquer the hedgerows. An ingenious sergeant by the name of Curtis Culin came up with the answer. Using steel from the German beach obstacles, he fashioned sharp scythe-like blades to be attached to the fronts of the tanks. These blades made it possible for the tanks to cut and gouge their way right through the hedgerows. Soon every American tank was equipped with Sergeant Culin's "rhino horns."

The Allied advance continued at a slow pace, however. Some members of the high command even feared that it might completely bog down into a foot-by-murderous-foot battle such as had taken place on the Western Front for several years during World War I. Pressure began to mount on Supreme Commander Eisenhower for a breakout from the beaches. It was at this point that Ike turned to General Patton for one of the victories the high-spirited armored leader "owed" the Allies.

Eleven

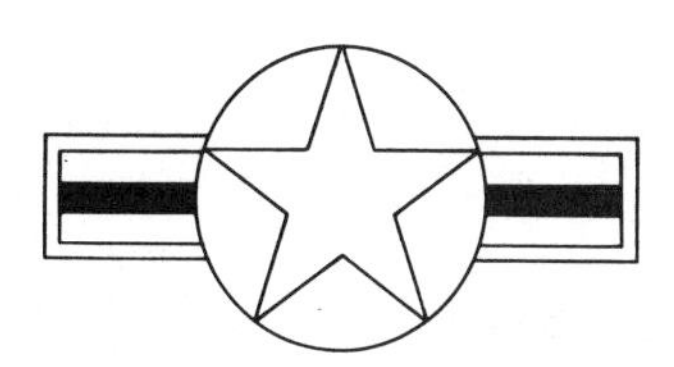

General Patton Pays off a Debt— with Interest

George Patton was one of the great generals in American military history. He was a great general, however, only in actual combat. When the pipes of peace played, Patton was at his worst — making unfortunate statements to the press, criticizing America's allies, and making himself generally disliked and difficult to deal with. But when the bugles of battle blew, Patton was at his best — and his best was very good indeed, as he was to prove on two occasions in the remaining months of war in Europe. The first was when he led the Third Army in its breakout from the Normandy beaches and the slashing armored drive across France that followed. The second came some months later when he led his armored columns to the rescue of surrounded American troops at beleaguered Bastogne in the Battle of the Bulge.

George Smith Patton, Jr., was born on a ranch at San Gabriel, California, on November 11, 1885. He attended school in Pasadena and then enrolled at Virginia Military Institute. Both his father, who was a lawyer, and his grandfather had been graduated from V.M.I. His grandfather had been a colonel in the Confederate Army in the Civil War.

In 1904 young George received an appointment to the United States Military Academy. He was graduated from West Point in 1909, having been named class adjutant, one of the Academy's two highest honors. Not a good student and too "cocky" to be popular, Patton was nevertheless admired as an athlete, marksman, and horseman. At the 1912 Olympic games in Stockholm, Sweden, he set a world's record in pistol shooting. In racing, swimming, and horsemanship he placed second.

Back on duty with the Army as a second lieutenant in the cavalry, Patton soon earned a reputation as an aggressive, attack-minded officer. After serving at a number of cavalry posts, he was sent to France in 1917 when the United States entered World War I. Here he became interested in the use of tanks in warfare when he saw the British use them at Cambrai. Later he organized an American tank brigade and took part in the St. Mihiel and Meuse-Argonne offensives. Severely wounded and left on the battlefield to die, Patton recovered and was awarded the Distinguished Service Cross for "conspicuous courage, coolness, energy, and intelligence in directing the advance of his brigade."

Between wars he bent all of his efforts toward mechanizing the United States Army Cavalry. When World War II began, he was named commander of the Second Armored Division at Fort Benning, Georgia, and promoted to brigadier general. Later he became commanding general of the First Armored Corps and continued to inject the spirit of

General George S. Patton, Jr. *(U.S. Army Photo)*

the hard-charging cavalry into his mechanized units. Soon they were the toughest and most feared outfits in the Army.

Patton's men seemed both to love and to hate him — but they were fiercely proud to be serving under him. They called him "Old Blood and Guts," and made jokes about the two pearl handled revolvers he always carried — but they knew he could outfight any of them. Well over six feet tall, General Patton was ramrod straight and every inch the fighting man. When he inspected several of his units before the invasion of North Africa, he told them in his curiously high and squeaky voice,

"Throw away your entrenching tools! We're not going to stop anywhere long enough to dig in! The only weapons you might need if you get out of your tanks are knives and bayonets. Sharpen them up and keep them sharp!"

After the successful invasion of North Africa, the Sultan of Morocco decorated Patton, and the inscription on the decoration read: *The lions in their dens tremble on hearing his approach.*

This was the man who had helped drive the Axis out of Africa and who spearheaded the capture of Sicily. And this was the man General Eisenhower was calling upon now to drive the Germans out of France. In the next ten months "Old Blood and Guts" was personally to lead the Third Army through half a dozen countries — France, Belgium, Luxembourg, Germany, Austria, and Czechoslovakia — capturing more than three-quarters of a million Germans and killing or wounding half a million more.

* * *

The breakout from the Normandy beachhead began on July 25, 1944. By this time the Allies had more than a million men in France, including thirteen American and eleven British divisions and one Canadian division.

At Caen and Caumont on the Allied left flank, the British and Canadian forces now launched a heavy attack. This was to draw as many German divisions as possible from the American First Army front at St. Lô on the Allied right flank. At the same time the U.S. Eighth and Ninth Air Forces and the R.A.F. sent 1,500 heavy bombers and hundreds of other planes to lay down a "carpet" of bombs in front of St. Lô. This aerial bombardment temporarily paralyzed the German defenders and the First Army was able to capture Avranches. It was here on August 1 that Patton's Third Army jumped off to exploit the breakthrough.

As the British continued to apply pressure on the left flank, Patton's armored divisions on the right flank raced around and toward the rear of the German armies. This maneuver was like the turning of a giant wheel: General Montgomery's forces at Caen and Caumont were the hub, and Patton's Third Army was the wheel rim turning to the left in the direction of Argentan.

In addition Patton sent several armored columns racing southward at a speed of some forty to fifty miles a day to capture Rennes, capital of Brittany, and the port city of St. Malo. This daring drive cut off the entire Brittany peninsula and isolated four German divisions. Within a week Patton had liberated more than 10,000 square miles of Nazi-held France. And the ironic part was that the American public did not even know that Patton was in France at this time! The movements of the Third Army were kept secret for days after it went into action. Finally U.S. newspapers began to print such headlines as "American Ghost Army Races Across France!" At this point SHAEF began to release stories on Patton's exploits. He was seldom out of the news again.

The German armies did not need any newspapers to tell them that *somebody* was threatening to destroy their entire strategy of defense. They reacted violently to Patton's encircling drive toward Argentan by counterattacking at

Mortain. They hoped to capture Mortain and drive ahead until they reached the Channel at Avranches and thus cut Patton's lifeline with the main Allied armies. With this threat to his rear, they did not think that Patton would continue to lead his unsupported armored columns deeper into their territory. Such a "naked" advance by mechanized units was unheard of, even by the famous German *panzers* conducting their *blitzkrieg* attacks. But Patton had a lesson or two to teach the Germans about lightning war.

Patton simply ignored the German counterattack at Mortain. He knew he could depend upon General Omar Bradley and General Courtney Hodges, who was now in charge of the First Army, to protect his rear. If they could not, then he would depend upon the Air Force to bring him supplies with air drops. As for his exposed flanks, he would also depend upon the Air Force to protect them. Using Ninth Air Force medium and attack bombers and R.A.F. rocket-firing Typhoons to bomb immediately ahead of his rampaging armored columns, Patton drove ahead as fearlessly as if he were supported on all sides by a dozen infantry divisions. By mid-August he had reached Argentan.

Meanwhile, as Patton drove toward Argentan, the British and Canadian forces captured Caen. They then advanced toward Falaise, which was just eighteen miles from Argentan. At this point General Bradley ordered Patton to stop his drive, because he was afraid Patton might accidentally go charging right into Montgomery's men.

Patton was furious when he received this order. He insisted he could capture Falaise and thus close the gap between that city and Argentan. If this were done they would have all of the German forces left in Normandy within their grasp. To stop now would mean losing most of them. Patton protested violently, but General Eisenhower confirmed Bradley's order.

Despite the fact that the bitter Patton had to bring his drive to a halt, the Germans found themselves in a gigantic trap. They were caught in a pincers between Patton on one side and the British and Canadians on the other with Bradley's and Hodges' armies pounding at them from the rear. The only escape route was through the narrow pincers of the Falaise-Argentan gap.

The Falaise gap turned into one of the great killing grounds of the war. Not only were the desperately fleeing Nazis attacked on all sides from the ground, but they were also relentlessly harried from the air. The Germans lost more than 50,000 prisoners and had some 10,000 men killed and at least 60,000 wounded. They also had more than 1,000 guns, tanks, and trucks destroyed. After the battle there was so much wrecked German equipment between Falaise and Argentan that the Allied armies had a difficult time making their way through it.

Patton lingered at Argentan only long enough to get the "Go!" signal from Bradley. Then he resolutely turned his tanks, halftracks, and other armored vehicles toward Paris and the Seine River and continued his pursuit of the fleeing Germans.

* * *

Meanwhile, on August 15, the Allies invaded southern France between Toulon and Nice. This amphibious assault was called "Anvil-Dragoon." At one time the Allied leaders had planned to invade the south of France even before invading Normandy. When Operation Overlord was decided upon, however, Anvil-Dragoon was postponed. Now General Eisenhower thought southern France should be invaded to protect the right flank of the Allied armies in Normandy and to secure additional ports.

In order to invade southern France, seven Allied divisions had to be taken out of Italy. British General Harold Alexander, commander of the Italian theater of war, and

U.S. General Mark Clark, commander of the American Fifth Army there, had been fighting under serious handicaps ever since Italy had been made a secondary front when Overlord was decided upon. Now, with the mounting of Anvil-Dragoon, the Italian campaign became even more difficult. Despite the withdrawal of seven of their best battle-tried divisions, however, Alexander and Clark continued their determined efforts to defeat the Germans in Italy.

Alexander was a greatly loved man and one of the war's great generals. A veteran of Dunkirk and the Tunisian desert fighting against Rommel, he was tremendously skilled at turning defeat into victory. He and Mark Clark had done just that at the end of the Italian winter and spring campaign of 1943-44.

Rome was one of the main goals in this campaign, and the Allied armies had advanced to within seventy-five miles of that ancient Holy City by the late autumn of 1943. There they had been stopped by a series of German defenses called the Winter or Gustav Line.

In January 1944 General Clark's forces tried to make an "end run" around the Winter Line with an amphibious landing at Anzio just thirty miles south of Rome. At first the landing seemed successful, but in a few days the Germans counterattacked strongly and the beachhead was threatened with disaster. Although the Allies managed to hang on at Anzio, it was several months before the six divisions there could break out of the beachhead. They were months of unbelievably grim fighting.

Elsewhere along the Winter Line the slugging match was equally brutal. Italy's mountainous countryside did not lend itself to open warfare, and the G.I.'s and Tommies had to doggedly capture one hill and then another and another — and yet another. And when they ran out of hills to assault, there was always one more river to cross. It was

Christmas Day dinner, 1943, was eaten off the hood of a jeep by these soldiers in Italy. (U.S. Army Photo)

Wherever they went, American G.I.'s helped and fed children. These riflemen are sharing their rations with an Italian boy at Anzio. (U.S. Army Photo)

at the Rapido River that the Thirty-sixth (Texas) Division under General Fred L. Walker suffered more than 2,000 casualties in a futile effort to ford the stream in the face of withering artillery and small arms fire. The Rapido was just one of several rivers that ran with Allied blood during the long and terrible months in Italy.

On top of one Italian mountain hillside was a Benedictine monastery named Monte Cassino. This monastery was a world-famous religious shrine, but it also stood directly in the path of the Allied advance. From its position high above the surrounding countryside the Germans could observe every move the Allies made. The Germans could also train their guns right down the throats of advancing riflemen. Finally, in February, it was decided that the monastery should be bombed. After warning leaflets were dropped to the Benedictine monks, several hundred B-17's and B-25's attacked the monastery. In this raid and several that followed severe damage was caused, but it was weeks before the Germans were driven from the Cassino mountain top. After the war General Clark admitted the bombing of Monte Cassino had been a mistake.

Air power was used heavily in the spring of 1944 to break the Italian stalemate. It was now that Alexander and Clark worked closely together to turn defeat into victory. In May, after weeks of intense aerial bombardment, the American Fifth Army and the British Eighth Army jumped off together and smashed the Winter Line. At the same time the Allies broke out of the Anzio beachhead. On June 4, just two days before the Overlord landings in Normandy, General Mark Clark and units of the Fifth Army had marched into Rome. It was the first Axis capital to fall.

The Germans, however, had still not given up in Italy. They retreated toward another system of fortifications, the Gothic Line, some 175 miles north of Rome. Alexander's

Monte Cassino, Italian Monastery. (U.S. Army Photo)

and Clark's men followed hard on the Germans' heels, capturing Leghorn and Perugia by mid-June. By August, shortly before Operation Anvil-Dragoon was launched against southern France, Florence was in Allied hands and the way lay clear ahead for the capture of Milan.

It would not be until May 1, 1945, however, that the Germans in Italy would surrender, marking the end of the Italian campaign — a campaign that cost the United States some 114,000 casualties. These casualties were not suffered in vain, however. The Italian campaign successfully tied down some twenty German divisions and kept them from fighting in France, where they might have turned the tide of Allied victory.

* * *

Operation Anvil-Dragoon was second in size only to Overlord. Almost 1,000 ships took part in it. The 60,000 assault troops were under the command of U.S. Generals Lucian K. Truscott and Alexander M. Patch. More than 1,300 Twelfth Air Force planes took part in the saturation bombing at dawn shortly before the assault. As at St. Lô, the aerial bombardment temporarily paralyzed the defenders who offered only slight resistance Within a few days the enemy was in full retreat up the Rhône Valley and being pressed hard by the Allied troops. Free French forces also joined in the pursuit. Soon the Anvil-Dragoon forces joined with General Patton's Third Army for the campaign into Germany.

Eisenhower moved his SHAEF headquarters to France in September shortly after the liberation of Paris. He now began to urge all of the Allied commanders under him to advance against the Germans on a broad front. At this point, however, the supply situation became critical. The Allies had more than three million men on the continent, and keeping them supplied with food, clothing, fuel, and ammunition became an almost impossible task.

One of the methods used to speed supplies to the combat areas was called the "Red Ball Express." This was a fast-moving truck service established by the U.S. Army. Every day some 9,000 trucks raced along at high speeds from Cherbourg to advanced supply dumps and depots. The Red Ball Express routes were all one-way roads, and the truck drivers were instructed not to stop for any reason whatsoever. Disabled vehicles were simply pushed off the roads. So effectively had the *Luftwaffe* been dealt with that Red Ball drivers could travel at night with their headlights on. As additional Mediterranean and English Channel ports were gradually cleared, the supply situation became less critical. In the north the British also captured the large port of Antwerp, but it was not ready for use until late November.

* * *

The Allied armies advanced abreast on a broad front toward the Rhine River during the late fall and winter of 1944. In doing so they were spread thin in some sectors. This was a risk that General Eisenhower was willing to take while his forces prepared for a final all-out drive to win the war in Europe.

Adolf Hitler, against the advice of his generals, now decided upon a last-gasp gamble with a counterattack in the weakly held Ardennes region. On the cold and stormy morning of December 16, some twenty-five German divisions suddenly smashed into the Allied lines. Thus began the epic Battle of the Bulge.

Twelve

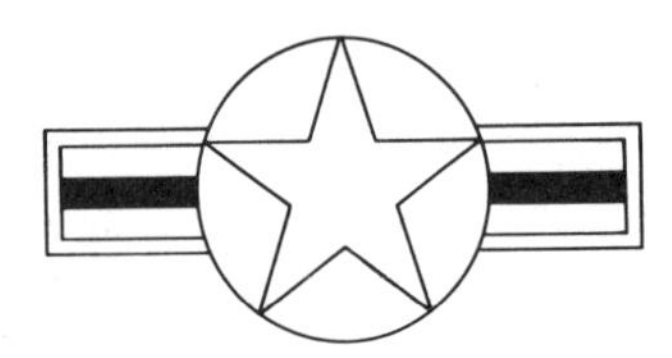

The Battle of the Bulge

Germany's sudden and powerful attack in the Ardennes forest region of Belgium caught the Allied armies completely by surprise. Germany had been on the defensive for so long that it seemed impossible for the Nazis suddenly to mount a major offensive.

The purpose of the Germans' Ardennes offensive was to recapture Antwerp and to destroy the British Twenty-first Army Group and the United States First and Ninth Armies. This would prolong the war for many months and perhaps give the Germans time to produce new secret miracle weapons like the V-1 and V-2. The *Luftwaffe* had also been showing signs of new life. It had begun using the first jet combat aircraft ever flown. If enough of these Messerschmitt ME-262 jets could be produced, the *Luftwaffe* might regain control of the air.

All was confusion behind the Allied lines when Field

Marshal Gerd von Rundstedt's *panzer* divisions first broke through the First and Ninth Army lines along a sixty-mile front. The main reason for this confusion was a secret offensive operation led by Germany's top spy, Otto Skorzeny. Skorzeny had been in charge of rescuing Mussolini from prison when the Fascist dictator had first been captured by Italian patriots. Now Skorzeny had an equally clever trick up his sleeve. This was Operation *Greif,* meaning "Grab."

Operation Grab was a Trojan Horse type of mission on which Skorzeny sent a special brigade of several hundred German Commandos behind the American lines. These Commandos spoke English, were dressed in captured American uniforms, and drove captured American vehicles. Their job was to disrupt all American activity by cutting telephone lines, directing troop traffic down the wrong roads, and doing everything possible to spread confusion and panic behind the lines.

German parachutists were also dropped in several areas just as the *panzer* divisions struck. Their job was to capture the bridges across the Meuse River before the Allies could destroy them. Although the parachutists did not succeed in their task, their presence added to the general chaos of the first few hours of the Ardennes breakthrough.

Soon all kinds of wild rumors began to race through the ranks of the G.I.'s from the Ardennes all the way back to Paris. One story was that English-speaking Germans dressed in American uniforms were on a special mission to kill General Eisenhower and other top Allied generals. One captured German Commando was found to have a picture of General Patton in his pocket, and this discovery gave strength to the rumor. In Paris Ike had such a strong security guard thrown around him that he could hardly conduct the defensive battle.

Closer to the front, infantrymen manning road blocks

stopped everybody and demanded they prove their identity. To do so they had to give the answers to special questions such as the names of American professional baseball players and teams, Hollywood movie stars, and U.S. Presidents. A good many American soldiers didn't know the answers to the questions. General Bradley himself had to admit to one trigger-happy G.I. that he didn't know who one famous movie star's husband was. Fortunately another G.I. recognized the general and he was allowed to pass.

Within twenty-four hours some degree of order was restored as rumors gave way to facts. But the facts themselves were not good. The German drive had already made a dangerous forty-five mile bulge in the American lines from Luxembourg in the south to St. Vith in the north. The Germans were moving so fast that they were not even bothering to take prisoners. When 160 Americans on the way to reinforce St. Vith were captured, the Nazi tank crews lined them up and machine-gunned them. One hundred forty G.I.'s were killed. The others escaped after pretending they were dead. They were able to return to the American lines and report what had happened. All of the G.I.'s in the area were fighting mad and eager to avenge the Malmedy massacre.

Despite valiant American efforts to plug the gap, von Rundstedt's armies seemed to be sweeping everything before them — or almost everything. In addition to St. Vith, one other major island of resistance had not given way before the sudden German onslaught. This was the town of Bastogne, the center of an important road network that was right in the path of the German Fifth *Panzer* Army. If the Tenth Armored Division with its big Sherman tanks could be reinforced and hold Bastogne, the entire timetable of the German advance would be upset. This was a spark of hope, and Ike acted to fan it into a flame.

The 101st Airborne Division was resting at Reims after weeks of frontline duty. Its commander, General Maxwell Taylor, was in the United States, but Ike ordered the 101st to Bastogne under its acting commander, General Anthony McAuliffe. By nightfall the airborne riflemen were speeding toward battle 11,000 strong. Despite the fact that they were in a combat zone, the convoys carrying the 101st drove through the dark with their headlights on.

Ike also ordered General Patton and his Third Army into the battle. Patton and British General Montgomery had never agreed with Ike that the Germans could be quickly defeated by a broad advance of all the Allied armies into Germany. Patton in particular had wanted to make a single sword-like thrust into Germany with his Third Army just as he had done in exploiting the breakthrough at St. Lô and Avranches. The slow slugging-match kind of fighting that resulted from advancing on a broad front did not appeal to Patton. Now he saw that the German breakthrough in the Ardennes had temporarily upset the Allied plan of battle, and he looked upon it as an opportunity for victory rather than as a defeat. This was his kind of fighting made to order.

"Let's let them get all the way to Paris," he told Ike. "Then we'll chop off their tail and surround them like we could have done at the Falaise gap."

This suggestions was never seriously considered.

"The Germans are not to get beyond the Meuse River!" Ike ordered. Then he also ordered Patton to the immediate relief of Bastogne.

Patton gladly accepted the challenge and in doing so he performed one of the miracles of maneuver of the war. The Third Army had been all set to attack in one direction through the German West Wall and into the Saar region. His armored columns and supply columns and communications systems were all set to jump off on that attack which had been scheduled for December 18. He now had to swing his entire army ninety degrees in the opposite direction to drive through Luxembourg. Not only did he have to perform the physical feat of changing the direction in which thousands of his men were to advance, but he also had to prepare and issue new battle maps to all of his units as well as give detailed orders for the new attack.

Many generals would have taken weeks to perform such a feat. Patton, however, did it almost overnight. Soon he was speeding the 125 miles to slash at the south flank of von Rundstedt's armies. To make the feat even more miraculous, it was performed in the midst of a blinding snowstorm. The Germans had not even taken Patton into consideration in their battle plans, because they thought he could not possibly figure in the fighting. Once again "Old Blood and Guts" fooled them.

By the time Patton was under way, however, the beleaguered battalions of the 101st Airborne Division were completely surrounded at Bastogne. The Germans assumed it was just a matter of time before the Americans would surrender. They would not have thought so if they had heard the conversation between two 101st riflemen.

"Hey, Mac, I hear they've got us surrounded."

"Yeah," his buddy said, "the poor jerks."

Two high-ranking German officers were sent into Bastogne carrying white flags of truce and a message. The message offered the Americans an opportunity to surrender — honorably. General McAuliffe read the message and then spoke for all of the men of Bastogne.

"Nuts!" he said.

The two German officers insisted they must have a written reply.

"What should I tell these guys?" General McAuliffe asked his aide, Colonel Joseph H. Harper.

"What you just said sounded pretty good to me," Colonel Harper said.

So General McAuliffe took a pencil and printed on the German surrender offer, "N-U-T-S!"

The two German officers read it and looked puzzled. Colonel Harper said, "If you don't know what 'Nuts!' means, it's the same thing as go to the devil. And I'll tell you something else. If you continue to attack, we'll kill every German who tries to break into the city!"

The Germans left.

By an odd coincidence, it was right at this time of year before the war that the Belgians had held their annual "Nuts Fair" in Bastogne, during which it was the custom for people to exchange gifts of nuts with one another. General McAuliffe was not aware of this, nor was he aware of the fact that his reply would immediately be headlined in newspapers throughout the world and go down in military history. After the war the people of Bastogne placed mementos of the siege in a building called "The Nuts Museum," where they are to be seen today.

When he learned of McAuliffe's reply, an enraged Hitler ordered von Rundstedt to throw every available division into the Bastogne battle. But the defiant 101st Airborne Division fought the Germans to a standstill.

And from the south, Patton's Third Army was now savagely smashing its way through the powerful German flank. Finally, on the day after Christmas, a thin wedge of an armored column of Third Army tanks punched its way into Bastogne. Patton had broken through.

The fight was still far from over. In fact some of the fiercest fighting of the Battle of the Bulge took place after Patton relieved the city. The object now was to widen the shoulders of the relief corridor by hammering back the Germans from both sides.

At this point, the Ninth Air Force and the Nineteenth

Tactical Air Command threw their weight into the conflict in an effort to turn the tide of battle. During most of the month of December the weather had been so bad that Ninth Air Force planes were weathered in. Soon after Patton's breakthrough, however, the bad weather lifted and within hours the sky was filled with more than 5,000 American planes.

Diving to tree-top level, the planes dropped their bombs directly on the *panzer* columns, and soon the Germans could no longer face the withering aerial bombardment. By the end of the month the Battle of the Bulge was over. By early January the Allies had recaptured all of the ground they had lost in the Ardennes.

Hitler's bold gamble was to prove fatal. Its only military result was to delay the end of the war by about six weeks. From a casualty standpoint, however, its effects were far greater. The United States suffered about 75,000 casualties, and the Germans about 100,000. Beyond that the Germans had used up their last reserves of manpower, equipment, and supplies. More than 600 German tanks, 1,600 planes, and 6,000 other vehicles were destroyed.

On January 12 the Americans and British had word that Russia had begun its long-awaited offensive all along the eastern front — an offensive whose final goal was to be Berlin. The handwriting of Germany's defeat was clearly written on the wall.

On March 15, the Presidential citation, the first in the United States history ever awarded a division, was personally presented by General Eisenhower to the 101st Airborne Division for "extraordinary heroism and gallantry in defense of the key communication center of Bastogne."

Meanwhile, on the other side of the world, the Americans in the Pacific and China-Burma-India theaters of war had also been writing a final chapter in the story of World War II: the defeat of Japan.

Thirteen

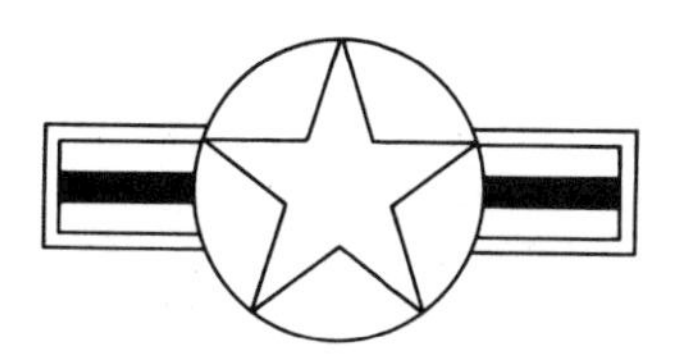

Merrill's Marauders

China-Burma-India, or "the C.B.I.," was something of a forgotten theater during most of World War II. Many soldiers made wry jokes about being "lost G.I.'s in the C.B.I," and General Marshall himself admitted that General Joseph Stilwell's men "were out at the end of the thinnest supply line of all." The demands of the war in Europe and the Pacific came first. Stilwell and his men could only have what was left. That wasn't much, but it didn't stop "Vinegar Joe" Stilwell. After being driven out of Burma early in the war, Stilwell had sworn he would return. The man who helped him keep his vow was General Frank D. Merrill.

General Merrill led a small but gallant band of about 3,000 G.I. jungle fighters who were trained to operate as a "long-range penetration group" behind enemy lines. Between February and May, 1944, these tough infantrymen marched and fought their way across several hundred miles of northern Burma. They were members of what the Army called "the 5,307th Composite Unit (Provisional)." They marched their way into legend, however, as "Merrill's Marauders." The Marauders' daring drive reached its climax with a bold bid to block a vital Japanese supply line and capture a key enemy airfield at Myitkyina (*mitch-in-ah*).

The Marauders were all men who had volunteered for "a dangerous and hazardous mission." This meant they probably would not return. Similar guerrilla units had already been organized by British General Orde C. Wingate. Wingate's "Chindits" (from a Burmese word meaning "lion") had gone on a raid into enemy-held Burma in 1943. While Wingate's Chindits suffered severe losses, the raid made the "forgotten men" of the C.B.I. feel that they were really taking part in the war for the first time.

Stilwell hoped to go a step further. If the Marauders could beat the Japanese at their own game in the jungles of Burma, Stilwell hoped that the Joint Chiefs of Staff would make the C.B.I. a main theater of war. But the Joint Chiefs had been firmly convinced since the beginning of the war that the best way to beat Japan was an island-hopping campaign across the Pacific. They wanted to give Stilwell enough help to keep China in the war, but not at the expense of the Pacific campaign.

The advance in the South Pacific had continued steadily after the successful Solomon Islands campaign, and General MacArthur had moved closer to his final goal — the recapture of the Philippines. Between June 1943 and July 1944 General Walter Krueger's Sixth Army made a series of leapfrogging attacks by land, sea, and air along the northern shore of New Guinea. This drive brought the Allies almost 1,500 miles closer to Japan and bypassed some 150,000 Japanese troops.

In the mid-Pacific campaign amphibious forces under

Admiral Chester W. Nimitz were now preparing to capture the Mariana Islands. From the Marianas B-20 Superfortresses — almost twice as big as the B-17's — could bombard the Japanese home islands.

Nimitz' drive across the central Pacific had begun in the autumn of 1943. Within a year the United States had regained complete control of the Pacific. Victory was bought, however, at a terrible cost in American lives.

The central Pacific campaign had started with "Operation Galvanic," the recapture of the Gilbert Islands. The twin keys to the Gilberts were Makin and Tarawa, two names that were to go down in U.S. Marine Corps history.

A shattering naval and aerial bombardment was intended to soften up the enemy defenses, but when the Marines stormed ashore at Makin and Tarawa they were met by a withering cross-fire. The Japanese were hidden in conccrete pillboxes and had to be dug out and defeated in hand-to-hand combat. Although the Japanese garrison on "terrible Tarawa" was small, it cost the Marines more than 3,000 casualties to capture the island in four days of some of the most savage fighting of the war.

"Operation Flintlock," the seizure of the Marshall Islands, came next. Here, too, the assault forces faced fanatical defenders, but this time the pre-invasion bombardment was so intense that there were few concrete pillboxes left standing. At Kwajalein and Eniwetok atolls the destruction reminded General Robert Richardson, veteran of World War I, of No Man's Land on the Western Front in 1917-18. In these grim engagements the Americans lost 700 men, while killing some 12,000 Japanese who fought almost to the last man.

In mid-February 1944, Japan's key naval base at Truk in the Caroline Islands was attacked by carrier aircraft and by B-24's based in the Admiralty Islands. No attempt was made to capture Truk. It was simply bypassed and its 75,-

000 defenders left behind, neutralized, just as had been done at Rabaul and in New Guinea.

As the Allied forces in the Pacific now got ready to close in on the Philippines, Okinawa, the Marianas, and Iwo Jima, Merrill's Marauders were meeting and defeating the veteran Japanese Eighteenth Infantry Division in a series of guerrilla engagements in the jungles of Burma.

* * *

Early in the war the Japanese had cut off the Burma Road, the only Allied land route to China. Beginning in 1943, General Stilwell made a determined effort to open a new overland route. American flyers were bringing in large amounts of supplies over the Himalayan Hump, but Stilwell was convinced that China could only be kept in the war with an even greater quantity of war materials supplied by land.

With American-trained Chinese combat troops leading the way, U.S. Army Engineers began to blast a new mountain route from Ledo in India to northern Burma. When the Ledo (later Stilwell) Road was finished, it would link up with a section of the old Burma Road and lead into China. The Marauders' job was to join with the Chinese combat troops in driving the Japanese out of northern Burma. This would make it possible for the engineers to complete the construction of the last sections of the Ledo Road.

General Merrill took command of the Marauders on January 4, 1944, shortly after they arrived in India. He told them at their first meeting, "General Stilwell expects us to be in Ledo within a month. From there we'll move out against the enemy." Then he added quietly, "We'll be the first American infantry outfit to fight in Asia since the Boxer rebellion in 1900. I don't have to tell you we've got a tradition to live up to."

The Marauders, many of whom were veterans of the jungle fighting on Guadalcanal, felt an immediate respect for Merrill. He was a tall, well-built soldier with graying sandy hair. He spoke softly with a cool New England voice, but there was a hard, no-nonsense ring to his words. They also soon learned that he knew as much as or more than they did about the Japanese. Not only did he speak Japanese fluently, but he knew exactly how the enemy fought.

General Frank Dow Merrill was now forty. He had been a Regular Army man since he was nineteen. Born in Hopkinton, Massachusetts, he had joined the Army as a private when he was unable to get an appointment to West Point. Working his way through the ranks to staff sergeant, he finally gained entrance to the military academy after taking the competitive examinations six times. The first five times he was turned down because he wore eyeglasses.

Graduated from West Point and commissioned a second lieutenant in 1929, Merrill later took a B.S. degree at M.I.T. During the 1930's he was sent to Japan as a military aide. There he went with the Japanese Army on their maneuvers and became acquainted with many young Japanese officers — the same men he was to fight against in World War II, including General Tanaka, commander of the Eighteenth Infantry Division.

By 1941 Merrill had been promoted to major and assigned as General MacArthur's intelligence officer in the Philippines. On Pearl Harbor Sunday he was in Rangoon on a mission for MacArthur. He remained there and became General Stilwell's chief of staff with the rank of brigadier general. When Stilwell had been run out of Burma by the Japanese in the spring of 1942, Merrill marched at his side into India. He was as determined to avenge that defeat as was "Vinegar Joe," and now he and his Marauders were about to do just that.

The first leg of the Marauders' march into Burma was not too difficult. Leaving India in February, they followed along the stretch of the Ledo Road that had already been completed. Mules were their main problem. Trucks could not be used to carry equipment through the jungles that lay ahead, so the Marauders had to use pack animals for this purpose. A shipment of 600 mules had been sunk on the way to India, and new animals had to be broken and trained for the job. Few of the Mauraders had ever been near a mule before, and now they had to be animal trainers as well as riflemen. Runaways were frequent during the early stages of the march, and the wild mules had to be rounded up and reloaded. This wasted much time and energy.

As soon as they left the Ledo Road, the Marauders' troubles began. Their first mission was to perform a hundred-mile circling maneuver and get behind the Japanese lines. In order to keep to the timetable set up by Stilwell they had to average twenty miles a day. To perform this feat they had to cut their way through thick forests of steel-hard bamboo trees that dulled knives after a few strokes. In addition, there were heavy rains that made the steep hills slick as ice slides. Men and animals struggled up hills a few inches at a time and then slid pell mell down the opposite slopes. Injuries were frequent and reloading the pack animals continued to be a problem.

Disease began almost immediately to take a fearful toll. Typhus, stomach trouble, and malaria struck down many of the men. In addition, leeches, poisonous snakes, leopards, and tigers were daily threats. Worst of all was the constant fear of being ambushed by Japanese jungle fighters who could remain completely hidden until the Marauders marched to within a few yards of concealed machine guns. The snapping of a twig often caused the Marauders to dive for cover.

Food was flown in by the Tenth Air Force from Assam in India. While the Marauders looked forward to these supply drops, they also dreaded them because the parachutes pointed out to the enemy exactly where the Americans were. After almost every air drop the Marauders had to fight a pitched battle with the Japanese before the march could continue.

Despite all of these obstacles, the Marauders held to their timetable. They did so by cutting their way relentlessly through the jungle for twelve hours a day. Finally they managed to make their way to a point several miles behind the enemy lines. When they reached this first goal they set up a roadblock and thus cut the Japanese supply line that ran through the Hukawng Valley. This trapped part of the Japanese Eighteenth Division between Merrill's Marauders and Stilwell's Chinese troops. More than 2,000 Japanese were killed in the battle that followed.

The first mission accomplished, Merrill now led his men in another "end run" for some seventy miles around the rear of another part of the Japanese forces. This march was made over heavily wooded mountains in an incredible three days. Arriving at the town of Shaduzup, the Marauders again set up a roadblock. The Japanese reacted by trying an "end run" of their own around the Marauders' flank. A long battle followed in which almost all of this part of General Tanaka's Eighteenth Division was destroyed.

In April General Merrill suffered a heart attack and had to be flown back to India. Later Stilwell let him return to combat, but once again he fell ill and had to be hospitalized.

By now the ranks of the Marauders had been severely thinned by combat casualties and disease. Nevertheless, they responded as valiantly as ever when they were ordered to capture the key Japanese airfield at Myitkyina. The capture of this airfield would make possible the completion of the overland route to China. It would also make it possible for more supplies to be flown over the Hump, since C-47's and C-54's could land en route to refuel.

Chinese troops joined with the Marauders for the attack on Myitkyina. This march took the American and Chinese guerrilla forces more than 100 miles over all but impassable jungle and mountain trails. On the way another series of battles was fought with the slowly retreating Japanese.

The rainy season, which normally would have ended all fighting in the theater, had now begun but the Marauders ignored it. They fought their way through ankle-deep mud and over mountain passes that ranged as high as 6,000 feet. Sometimes these mountains were so steep the men crawled up them on their hands and knees. Occasionally men and pack animals slipped over precipices and fell to their death below. For periods as long as two days at a time, they fought without food or water.

The Marauders reached Myitkyina in mid-May. Using a plan of attack developed by Merrill and Stilwell, several columns of Marauders and Chinese knifed their way through the Japanese lines and then swiftly fanned out in different directions. A flaming battle at close quarters followed, but on May 17 the airfield was captured. Almost immediately Allied reinforcements and equipment began to be flown in from India for the attack on the nearby city of Myitkyina itself, the largest city in northern Burma.

Of the 3,000 Marauders who had begun the campaign only half were left when the Myitkyina airfield fell. Because of disease, those that remained had to be flown back to India at the rate of 100 a day. By the end of May only about 200 Marauders were left to take part in the attack on the city, which was captured on August 3. It had been "a dangerous and hazardous mission" indeed, and one from which too few Marauders returned.

The Marauders' accomplishments in fighting five major and thirty minor battles were summed up by the Distinguished Unit Citation which they were awarded. It read:

> AFTER A SERIES OF SUCCESSFUL ENGAGEMENTS IN THE HUKAWNG AND MOGAUNG VALLEYS OF NORTHERN BURMA IN MARCH AND APRIL 1944, THE UNIT WAS CALLED ON TO LEAD A MARCH OVER JUNGLE TRAILS THROUGH EXTREMELY DIFFICULT MOUNTAIN TERRAIN AGAINST STUBBORN RESISTANCE IN A SURPRISE ATTACK ON MYITKYINA. THE UNIT PROVED EQUAL TO ITS TASK AND AFTER A BRILLIANT OPERATION OF 17 MAY 1944 SEIZED THE AIRFIELD AT MYITKYINA, AN OBJECTIVE OF GREAT TACTICAL IMPORTANCE IN THE CAMPAIGN, AND ASSISTED IN THE CAPTURE OF THE TOWN OF MYITKYINA ON 3 AUGUST 1944.

The small group of surviving Marauders was disbanded on August 10, 1944. Neither they nor the lessons they learned were forgotten, however. Today's United States Army has a guerrilla organization called "Special Forces." Merrill's Marauders proved that each soldier had to be a one-man army to fight behind the enemy lines. Modern Special Forces soldiers make sure they are unbelievably tough both mentally and physically by undergoing the most severe kind of training at the Army's special warfare center at Fort Bragg, North Carolina.

One of the training methods is unarmed combat in the so-called "Gladiator Pit." The Gladiator Pit is a huge hole in the ground six feet deep where sixty-man free-for-alls are held just for the fun of it.

In their training, and in actual guerrilla combat against the Reds in such places as Southeast Asia, the modern Special Forces soldiers continue to live up to the words of one of Merrill's Marauders, Lieutenant Charlton Ogburn, Jr. At the end of the campaign in northern Burma Ogburn said, "Above everything else, courage is what counts."

Fourteen

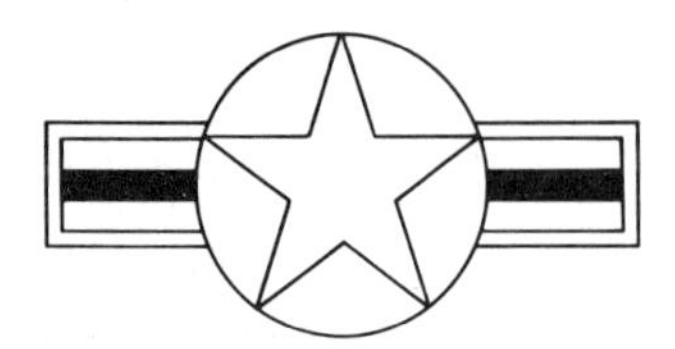

Kilroy Comes Home

Late on the wintry afternoon of March 7, 1945, units of the First Army's Ninth Armored Division battled their way into the city of Remagen, Germany. Spearheading the attack was a squad of veteran American riflemen led by Sergeant Alexander Drabik. Drabik led his men to the bank of the Rhine River, where he was surprised to find the Ludendorff Bridge still intact. Everyone had assumed the retreating Germans would destroy all of the bridges across the Rhine and thus seriously delay the American advance into the heart of Germany. Here was a prize that could shorten the war by several months and save thousands of lives!

Drabik knew the bridge must be loaded with charges of dynamite set to explode at any minute, but he did not hesitate. Pumping his right arm rapidly up and down in the infantry "follow-me-on-the-double" signal, Drabik raced across the bridge in the face of severe small-arms fire. Halfway across they felt the bridge tremble as one of the small dynamite charges exploded, but the bridge held. Reaching the other side, they seized the Germans who were just about to set off the main charges. Army engineers now followed Drabik and his men and cut the wires of the main charges. Soon additional infantrymen also followed and by nightfall the opposite bank of the Rhine was occupied in force.

The First Army thus became the first Allied army to cross the Rhine in World War II. Within two weeks some 100,000 men and tens of thousands of tons of equipment and supplies had poured across the Ludendorff Bridge. It wasn't until some time later that an interrogation officer told Sergeant Drabik that German prisoners of war had revealed that the main charges of dynamite had been set to explode just ten minutes after the sergeant and his valiant squad of men had raced across the bridge.

By the end of March all of the Allied armies had crossed the Rhine and were slashing their way into the heart of Germany. During the first three weeks of April, the Allies captured more than 300,000 German prisoners in the Ruhr Valley alone.

Meanwhile, the Russians were continuing their massive assault all along the eastern front. The Red Army had crossed the German borders in late January and was just sixty miles from Berlin by mid-March.

The Allies now fanned out in all directions and smothered all German resistance. Mass surrenders were so frequent that many Allied divisions were hard pressed to take care of prisoners.

Russia began its final assault on Berlin in April and soon had surrounded the city. Inside the capital, the cornered Adolf Hitler lived out his last days like an animal in the air raid shelter of his Chancellery. This concrete bunker was buried fifty feet below the ground. Hitler still believed a miracle would occur to deliver him and the German people from their fate. He talked almost hourly with his faithful propaganda minister, Joseph Goebbels, who kept telling the Führer that according to an astrologer's horoscope Hitler's stars indicated that Germany was still destined to win the war. On April 12 word was received in the bunker that President Franklin D. Roosevelt had died, and Goebbels gleefully reported this fact to the mad Nazi leader. This was a certain sign, Goebbels said, that the horoscope was right: Hitler would outlive all of his enemies and rule the world. For the moment the hysterical Hitler himself took heart — even as the Allied world mourned its lost leader, the architect of a victory he had not lived to see.

Soon Soviet artillery shells were exploding within yards of Hitler's underground trap, and the Führer himself finally realized that his fate was sealed. On April 30 Hitler, who had just turned 56, first killed his favorite dog, Blondi, and then urged Eva Braun to commit suicide. Eva had been a notorious friend of Hitler's for many years and had recently become his legal wife. She now killed herself by taking poison, and a short time later Hitler shot himself. Their bodies were taken outside the bunker by Hitler's aides, gasoline was poured over them, and they were set on fire. Hitler had boasted his Third Reich would last for a thousand years. It had lasted just slightly more than twelve — but they were twelve of the blackest years in human history.

Two days earlier, Mussolini had been assassinated by Italian partisans outside Milan. He was then taken into the city and hung up by the heels in front of a butcher shop. On April 29, all the remaining German forces in Italy had surrendered.

There was now no organized German government, and

various Nazi leaders tried desperately to surrender what was left of the nation's fighting forces. Finally on May 7 General Alfred Jodl, German Army Chief of Staff, and Admiral Hans von Friedeburg, German Navy Commander in Chief, asked for peace terms. The Allies offered the Nazis the same terms they had been offered since early in the war: unconditional surrender.

The surrender was signed at General Eisenhower's headquarters, a little red schoolhouse at Reims, France, on May 7, 1945. President Harry S. Truman proclaimed May 8, 1945, as Victory in Europe (V.E.) Day.

* * *

During the final months of the war in Europe, the war in the Pacific was also drawing to a close. McArthur made good his "I shall return!" promise when his forces landed at Lingayen Gulf in Luzon early in 1945. Earlier, the U.S. Sixth Army had invaded the east coast of Leyte. In reconquering the Philippines MacArthur's men followed exactly the route used by the Japanese in their conquest several years earlier. Manila was recaptured in early March, but scattered resistance continued throughout the islands for several months.

By now Saipan, Guam, and Tinian in the Marianas had been taken by Admiral Nimitz' forces, and it became possible to attack Japan from the air. Many B-29's were lost in the sea on the long return flight from Japan to the Marianas, however, and it was decided to seize an island closer to Japan for emergency landings. This was Iwo Jima.

It was thought that Iwo Jima could be captured in a few days. It actually took a month, and Marine casualties amounted to almost 20,000 men, 5,000 of whom were killed, the heaviest casualty rate in any invasion of an island during the war.

This Japanese dummy tank carved out of volcanic ash on Iwo Jima successfully drew American fire. (U.S. Army Photo)

The capture of Iwo Jima also saved many lives. About 2,500 B-29 Super-fortresses carrying some 25,000 men made emergency landings there. Fleet Admiral King said that the lives that were thus saved "far exceeded the lives lost in the capture of the island."

The Twentieth Air Force Bomber Command under General Curtis LeMay next tried low-level "fire-bombing" attacks on Japan. A single raid in early March burned out sixteen square miles of the center of Tokyo, killing 80,000 people and destroying more than a quarter of the city's flimsy wooden buildings. Several similar raids followed.

Early in April an American amphibious assault was launched against Okinawa in the Ryukyu Islands. The Ryukyus were on the doorstep of Japan, and the enemy defended them fanatically. The campaign lasted until June, and American casualties were heavy both on land and at sea.

At sea the Japanese Air Force sent suicide pilots (*Kamikazes*) to dive their bombers into U.S. ships deliberately. Some twenty-five American ships were sunk by the *Kamikaze (divine wind)* pilots, 175 were damaged, and the U.S. Navy suffered almost 35,000 casualties.

Late in July President Truman, Prime Minister Churchill, and Premier Stalin met at Potsdam, Germany to discuss postwar plans for Europe and to decide the best way to end the war with Japan. Just before this conference, President Truman had word that American scientists had succeeded in exploding an experimental atomic bomb at Alamogordo, New Mexico. This bomb was the end result of the Manhattan Project which had been started early in the war. Although more than 100,000 people had been working on various parts of this project, only a handful had known what its purpose was.

When President Truman learned of the successful results

Fanatical Japanese often had to be blasted out of their defensive positions on Okinawa. (U.S. Army Photo)

in New Mexico, he immediately told Churchill and Stalin the news. Stalin seemed unimpressed, but Churchill was immediately aware that the successful explosion of the bomb at Alamogordo had ushered in a new, atomic age. The three leaders then agreed to send word to Kantaro Suzuki, Japan's Premier, to surrender or face complete destruction. Suzuki defied the Allies to continue the war. His defiance left President Truman little choice but to use the best method of ending the war with the least possible loss of life.

On August 6, 1945, the first atomic bomb was dropped on Hiroshima from the B-29 *Enola Gay,* piloted by Colonel Paul Tibbets, Jr. Colonel Tibbets was the same pilot who had flown General Eisenhower's plane to Gibraltar at the beginning of the invasion of North Africa. The *Enola Gay* was named for Tibbets' mother. The Hiroshima bomb destroyed five square miles in the center of the city, killing between 70,000 and 100,000 people. On August 9 a second atom bomb was dropped on Nagasaki from the B-29 *Bock's Car* piloted by Major Charles W. Sweeney.

Two days after most of Hiroshima was destroyed, Russia entered the war against Japan, a move Stalin had agreed to make at a meeting of the Allied leaders at Yalta in the Crimea some months earlier. At that time Russia's declaration of war against Japan had seemed desirable. Now, however, it was clear that Japan was in a state of near-collapse and Russia could only be entering the war to share in the spoils.

Russian forces quickly overran Manchuria and, in a move that was to have far-reaching results in the future, occupied the northern half of Korea. It was agreed by the Allies that as soon as the war ended, Japanese forces in northern Korea would surrender to Russia and those in the south of Korea would surrender to the United States.

Atom bombs dropped at Hiroshima and Nagasaki caused Japan to sue for peace. (U.S. Army Photo)

This arrangement, so lightly made at the time, was to lead to the Korean War less than five years later.

On August 10 the Japanese government offered to surrender. General MacArthur and Admiral Nimitz met the Japanese envoys on September 2 aboard the battleship *Missouri* in Tokyo Bay and the official surrender was signed. The long-awaited Victory over Japan (V.J.) Day had arrived. World War II was over.

* * *

All during the war there had been one important member of the United States Armed Forces no one had ever actually seen. Although no one had ever seen him, everybody in the Army, Navy, and Air Force knew this mystery figure had fought by their side to defeat Germany and Japan. This legendary warrior had been wherever there were American men fighting this great global war. He had always made certain that his presence would be noted by leaving behind him a message that read "Kilroy was here!"

From the jungles of the South Pacific to the air war over Europe the famed Kilroy fought his way into American folklore alongside such heroes as Paul Bunyan and Pecos Bill. When the first Flying Fortresses landed in England he must have been on hand because his message was scrawled across the nose of one of the bombers. At Guadalcanal, and Midway, and in North Africa when America's first victories were won, Kilroy's name was found on maps and orders and in many battle reports. From training grounds in the United States to battlegrounds on the continent of Europe and the coral islands of the Pacific there appeared such messages as, "Kilroy ate chow here," "Kilroy slept here," "Kilroy's girl lives near here," "Kilroy landed here," "Kilroy fought here."

Exactly where or how the legend of Kilroy began is not known. His messages were probably first carried around the world in the early days of the war by the Army Transport Command, which flew to all corners of the globe. This would have been the fastest way to spread the catchy, "Kilroy was here!" line once it began to be used in the United States.

James J. Kilroy of Halifax, Massachusetts, did claim that he was actually the one who started the Kilroy legend. James Kilroy said that while working as an inspector at the Bethlehem Steel Company's Quincy, Massachusetts, shipyard he wanted to let his boss know he was doing his job so he scrawled, "Kilroy was here!" in yellow chalk on the work he had inspected. There were other real-life Kilroys, however, in other parts of the United States who also said they had first written the words.

Wherever the Kilroy legend began, it was typically American. Kilroy overcame impossible odds, defeated time and distance, was everywhere and did everything at the same time, and conquered all enemies. It had taken just such an effort to win the war. Kilroy was the spirit of America's fighting forces on land, at sea, and in the air, forces which had started out a mere handful of untrained civilians and ended up some fifteen million seasoned veterans. And now, with victory in Europe and the Pacific finally won, America's millions of Kilroys began the long voyages back to their homes and home towns.

There were hundreds of thousands who had helped write the Kilroy legend in distant outposts who would not return home. These were the brave dead. There were also almost three-quarters of a million Kilroys who would bear the scars of battle all their lives. World War II was the most costly in human life of any war in which the United States had ever engaged. Like the story of Kilroy, however, the price that the nation's fighting forces paid and the final victory they won would live on in the hearts and minds of all Americans.

Books About World War II

The Army Almanac (Stackpole Company, 1959).
Bullock, Alan, *Hitler: A Study in Tyranny* (Harper, 1960).
Caidin, Martin, *Black Thursday* (Dutton, 1960).
Collier, Richard, *The Sands of Dunkirk* (Dutton, 1961).
Compton's Pictured Encyclopedia (F. E. Compton). Article on World War II and related biographies.
Cunningham, W. Scott and Sims, Lydel, *Wake Island Command* (Little, 1961).
Devereux, James, *The Story of Wake Island* (Lippincott, 1947).
Divine, David, *The Nine Days of Dunkirk* (Norton, 1959).
Dupuy, R. Ernest, *The Compact History of the United States Army* (Hawthorn, 1956).
Eisenhower, Dwight D., *Crusade in Europe* (Doubleday, 1948).
Esposito, Vincent J., *The West Point Atlas of American Wars: Vol. 2 1900-1953* (Praeger, 1959).
Fleming, Peter, *Operation Sea Lion* (Simon & Schuster, 1957).
Gurney, Gene, *Five Down and Glory: A History of the American Air Ace* (Putnam, 1958).
Life Picture History of World War II (Simon & Schuster, 1950).
Lord, Walter, *Day of Infamy* (Holt, 1957).
McKee, Alexander, *Black Saturday* (Holt, 1960).
Masters, John, *The Road Past Mandalay* (Harper, 1961).
Merriam, Robert E., *Dark December: The Full Account of the Battle of the Bulge* (Ziff-Davis, 1947).
Meyer, Robert, Jr., *The Stars and Stripes Story of World War II* (McKay, 1960).

Millis, Walter. *This is Pearl! The United States and Japan* (Morrow, 1947).
Morison, Samuel Eliot, *The Struggle for Guadalcanal: August 1942-February 1943* (Little, 1949).
Ogburn, Charlton, Jr., *The Marauders* (Harper, 1959).
Phillips, C. E. Lucas, *The Greatest Raid of All* (Little, 1960).
Potter, E. B., ed., *The United States and World Sea Power* (Prentice-Hall, 1955).
Reynolds, Quentin, *The Amazing Mr. Doolittle* (Appleton, 1953).
Richards, Denis and Saunders, H. St. G., *Royal Air Force: 1939-1945* 3 vols. (British Information Services, 1954).
Rickenbacker, Edward V., *Seven Came Through* (Doubleday, 1943).
Ryan, Cornelius, *The Longest Day: June 6, 1944* (Simon & Schuster, 1959).
Scott, Robert L., Jr., *Flying Tiger: Chennault of China* (Doubleday, 1959).
Shirer, William L., *The Rise and Fall of the Third Reich* (Simon & Schuster, 1960).
Slim, William J., *Defeat Into Victory* (McKay, 1961).
Snyder, Louis L., *The War: A Concise History, 1939-1945* (Messner, 1960).
Stilwell, Joseph W., *The Stilwell Papers* (Sloane, 1948).
Thomas, Hugh, *The Spanish Civil War* (Harper, 1961).
Thompson, R. W., *At Whatever Cost: The Story of the Dieppe Raid* (Coward-McCann, 1957).
White, William L., *They Were Expendable* (Harcourt, 1942).
Whitehouse, A.G.J., *The Years of the War Birds* (Doubleday, 1960).
Wilmot, Chester, *The Struggle for Europe* (Harper, 1952).
U.S. Department of the Army, Office of the Chief of Military History, *Chronology: 1941-1945* (Government Printing Office, 1960).
—— *Cross-Channel Attack* (Government Printing Office, 1951).
U.S. Navy Department, Naval History Division, *United States Naval Chronology: World War II* (Government Printing Office, 1955).
U.S. War Department, Historical Division, *Omaha Beachhead 6 June-13 June 1944* (Government Printing Office, 1945).

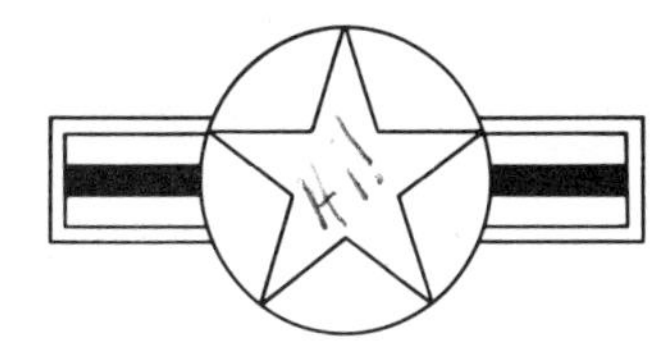

Index